Kaspoit!

*"Everyone carries a shadow, and the less it is embodied
in the individual's conscious life, the blacker
and denser it is."*
—CARL JUNG

Kaspoit!

(a novel)

DENNIS E. BOLEN

ANVIL PRESS | VANCOUVER

Anvil Press Publishers Inc.
P.O. Box 3008, Main Post Office
Vancouver, B.C. V6B 3X5 CANADA
www.anvilpress.com

Library and Archives Canada Cataloguing in Publication

Bolen, Dennis E. (Dennis Edward), 1953-
Kaspoit! / Dennis E. Bolen.

ISBN 978-1-897535-05-9

I. Title.
PS8553.O4755K37 2009   C813'.54   C2009-904205-3

Printed and bound in Canada
Cover design by Derek von Essen
Back cover photo: Edward Morrison
Interior design by HeimatHouse

Represented in Canada by the Literary Press Group
Distributed by the University of Toronto Press

The publisher gratefully acknowledges the financial assistance of the Canada Council for the Arts, the Book Publishing Industry Development Program (BPIDP), and the Province of British Columbia through the B.C. Arts Council and the Book Publishing Tax Credit.

In Memory of

Louise Pargeter

Kaspoit! (ka-'spȯit) Function: *noun*; Etymology: imitative; Date: 2009; Definition: the natural noise of a beer can being opened. — *Kaspoit!* intransitive verb.

Night; fireside: HulkSpeak

Open that fucken beer.
I gotta finish this one.
Throw it in the fucken fire. Musta gone flat by now.
Whyda fuck you care?
Cause when you open that one then we'll be officially out.
An you bein the junior member round here.
Gotta go get more beer.
Right.
Well here. Take the fucken thing.
Doen mind if I do. Thought you'd never figger it out.
Fucken smart guy.
Kaspoit!
Ahhh. *SwillGulp*. Still nice an cold.
Oughta be. Fucken freezin out here.
Stand close to the flame.
Damn near roastin my dick off as it is.
An yer back is freezin right?
You got it.
Part of a proud tradition.
Yeah. *SwillGulp*. Guess it's okay.
Effen eh it's okay.
You sure like it eh Gort.
Fucken sure do.
KnottyFir crackleBurn.
Whadya do before?
SweepArm. Whad anya these fuckheads do before?
LeatherBulk blackStand fireThrong.
I guess eh.
Fucken right you guess.
Yeah.

S'not what's important. *SwillGulp*. Important's what we're doin now.

Gotcha.

Heard about Scroaty?

Naw. What?

Speakina what's important. His ol lady damn near snuffed the fucken guy.

No fucken way.

Fucken dumbass left his gun out where she could grab it.

Naw.

He's okay. *SniggerCackle*. Grabbed it away before she could get off a second shot.

She fucken fired at im?

She was all fucken scared up the ass cause he didn't come home. Got held up in that thing southa the border.

So she got all paranoid.

Effen eh. Thought he was never comin home. Thought either the cops or us guys might come through the door and try to whack er right there. Fucken loser bitch.

I can see the cops dickin with er. But whyda fuck would we fucken care?

Zackly. But. There's no figgerin the female mind.

I tuck away my ordinance like it was treasure.

Well sure. You gotta take precaution.

Effen eh.

I mean I got a fucken kid wanderin around. Hell knows what he'd get up to.

Just common sense.

Absòfuckenlutely.

So. *SwillGulp*. He's back home an everythin's cool?

Naw naw. That's the rilly crazy part. What I hear is he's out on his fucken ear.

What? She pull a pistol outta her snatch or sumpm?

Naw. He disarmed her good I magine. Nope. Ol Scroat just

couldn't stand the natter. Got fed up of the neverending fucken female fanfare. Moved back out to the ol homestead.

Not that fucken dive.

Yup. Big change. Fancy fucken three storey condo town-house to brokedown shithouse chickenfarm in one foul swoop. Helluva comedown. But whattya gonna do?

I guess.

He'll figger it out.

Oh yeah.

UniLift swillGulp.

Fuck. *ShiverHulk.*

Yeah fuck.

Fuck yeah.

ChuckleHulk.

Any case. That's a whole lotta wacky shit.

Guess she got tireda havin chunksa fruit an vegetables shoved up her ass.

Huh?

Long story. *HulkSnort.* Short dick.

Oh yeah?

Don't tellim I said that.

Fuck me Gort I'm not gonna talk about anya this shit.

Smart. Guess you could say that's why we talk out here fire-side different than we talk inside.

Logical.

If it was it'd be the first thing I said today that was. I hate thinkin.

Know what you mean. Always gets me in trouble.

There ya go.

Hah.

Hah hah. *SwillGulp.*

ShudderHulk. Think I'm gonna go inside.

Drink more. *GloomPeer.* Hey Geek!

Huh? *HulkSwivel.* Gort? What?

Chuck us a beer.
Get yer own fucken beer.
You got four hangin from that cluster there.
Yeah. So?
We're havin a conversation here.
Oh fuck. *CanToss. CanToss.*
OneHand beerCatch. Good man. *Kaspoit!*
Kaspoit!
GulpChug huffBreath.
Jeeze. *CanPoint.* Those houses are gettin close.
Huh. Real estate man.
Eh?
Developers.
Livin so close to here.
Only ten acres. The whole place.
Not far enough.
They don't know man.
They fucken well better not man.
HulkLaugh.
They'd shit!
LaughHulk.
Besides. It fucken stinks here.
It's a fucken farm.
There's hardly any animals.
Cep Friendly and Stew and their skankbitch sister.
Effen eh.
Fuck it's fucken amazin to me.
What the whole Friendly family setup?
Yeah. Such a crowda scungerats.
No worse than yer usual trailerpark walkin garbawj.
Aw fuck though. Stupid?
Yeah there's that.
As the fucken night is long.
Onea the eight fucken wondersa the whitetrash world.
Go figger.

What I gotta do is go in. Fucken freezin.
Pussy.
Yeah that too.
What time is it?
Time to fucken go in Gort.
Not even midnight.
Late enough for me. What is it? Minus ten?
Nowhere near. Who gives a shit?
I do. *FeetStamp*. Gotta get warm. *TossEmpty fireHiss*. And.
Gotta find me some wet cunt.
Friendly back yet?
He better.
Okay. Gotta piss though.
Me too.
So cold I'm gettin a hardon.
Me too. *TossCan*.
GlistenArc fireHiss.

SmokeShadow fileWalk.
CorrugaMetal rustQuonset liquorShed.
OpenDoor.
TalkFrenzy bodySteam hulkSweat reekBreath nicoMari smoke-Hang.
Stew.
BarTend headNod. Hey Gort.
Hey yerself.
How many?
Six or so.
Hah hah. *FridgeBend*. Kinda early.
Too effen cold out there. Must be minus fifteen.
Gettin old Gort?
Fuck you.
Not til the girls are finished with me.
Fucken smart guy.
I could never keep up with you Gort.

Nevermind all the smallshit talktalk. Where's the girls?
Friendly's not back yet.
What?
He's not here.
Why the fuck not?
Bitches are gettin tougher to find. *SixPack slapBar.* The
good ones.
What's to find? You drive up. You say Hey Bitch.
They take your plate number now I hear.
Only if you're dumb enough to use your own car.
We ain't got no other car.
Well fucken get a couple. What about the wrecking yard?
Nonea them are runnin.
Look the fuck around. Nothin but fucken mechanics in the
room.
Friendly don't like nobody touchin em.
Well there you go. Fucken retard.
Aw he's not that bad. Gets the jobs done.
Everybody knows how dumb Friendly is. Talkin to himself.
Hmmm. If you say so Gort. I'm just slingin booze.
See that you keep slingin. *Kaspoit!* And find out where the
fucken hookermobile is.
Gotcha.
HulkLurch drinkWalk.
Hey Gort. *TableMonster.* Where's the bitches?
Not here.
What?
Patience Geeksterman. Have a beer.
Fuck patience. *Kaspoit!* What's the matter with Friendly?
Other than being fucked in the brain?
HulkLaugh.
A guy's gotta keep his hardon.
Don't go home with your hardon.
MonsterGroup talkJam.
Naw. Keep it here.

Get rid of it here.
Yeah okay. So when's the chicks gonna come?
Never. Unless you take too long to fuck em.
Hardy har. You know what I mean.
Friendly's out getting em.
Where the fuck is he?
Where the fuck else?
Whereabouts is Scroaty?
In the can. I guess.
Where you goin after?
I'm goin the fuck home. But not yet. Not before I get my dick off.
Home eh?
Wherethefuck else?
What kinda wheels you got nowadays?
Vette.
You seen my cruiser?
That green piecea shit?
Got a fucken Blaupunkt in er. Man. Hundred watts on six sides. Blow yer ears off yer fucken head.
Whoopee shit. Don't want my fucken ears blown off my fucken head.
GoofLook. LeerSneer. BlackJean hulkSit.
MonsterLurch.
Scroaty. Howareya?
The shits Geekster. *Kaspoit!* How the fuck are you?
Fucken fine.
Still driving that green piecea shit?
Hyuck.
Aw you guys.
Yera fucken peasant Geek. *Kaspoit!* Don't try to tell us about wheels.
You guys are too fucken stupid to understand anyway.
Fuck you.
Fuck you asshole.

HalfSpeed canFling spewFly.
JoltLeg jostleStand.
TableTilt canStream.
Pack it up you a-holes! *BarTend megaCall.*
CanFly punchThrow.
Friendly's here!
TussleMonster hulkHead knuckleRam.
HulkSwing skullWhack.
Goddamnit! *BarTend megaLoud.* The whores are here. Go off and fuck this out!
FightFlag.
MonsterSpit. CanGrip gaspGuzzle.
GirdFurrow.
HulkChug. SudSpew.
Did somebody say hookers?
Fucken eh. *GumBoot coverAll mudMan.* They're here.
Friendly. It's about fucken time.
Hello to you too Gort.
Don't get smart.
Howdy Geek.
Friendly.
Scroat.
What kept ya?
Nothin kept me. I'm here ain't I?
How many'd ya get?
Five.
Five?
Yeah.
Not enough.
Well it's gonna hafta be.
What's the fucken problem?
They're gettin skittish.
Yeah. Probly the smell. No wonder. You could use a wash. And comb your hair for fucksakes.
Why don't you?

Not my job gofer. Get it?

Ta heck with you.

Fuck you too.

What were you guys fightin about?

Fightin?

Yeah.

Were we fightin?

You wacky guys.

This place is gettin kinda boring.

My mom used to say only borin people get bored.

Well if your mom was here we'd fuck er and make er wash our cars. Where's the girls?

Usual place.

I told you to change it. *StoneStern*. What about the back room?

What's the matter with the girlmobile?

It stinks to high shit in there.

It's good enough.

For you maybe. *HulkSwill. Kaspoit!*

ShagHead shakeSmile. You guys are sumpm.

Sumpm bettern you dickhead.

HulkLurch.

Hey. *RiseMove.* Chicktime.

OuterDark rangeFile.

FireCircle.

StopPause. Hey Geek. *FriskPat pocketLeather.* Where's the joint in there?

Donno if I got one.

What the fuck.

Ask these guys.

Hey. Anybody got smoke?

WordFree handReach.

Thanks bro.

TokeMonster.

HulkToke.
TokeToke.
HoldBreath steamNostril faceFume.
TokeToke.
GulpGlug canToss.
Effin. *HulkHack.* Where's this shit from? *HackRasp.* Shitville?
Fuck you.

Look me up. *SmokeToke.* I'll get you sumpm won't rip out
your linings.

Heh heh.

RackHack. Awk. *StoneStagger.*

Whassamatter?

Some shit in there bro.

Yer lookin kinda green.

Came on likea thunderbolt from shit hell. *RackHack.*

Didn't hit me that bad.

I'm fucken seein double. *RackHack.* Can't be the beer.

Aw yer getting soft in yer old age.

Fuck me. *HackRasp.*

It's your coughin. Don't cough. Only pussies cough.

Can't fucken. *RackHack.* Stop it.

You gotta man up there Gort.

Oh fuck. *HulkGut spewToss.*

HissFire.

Fucken gross.

Fuck. *RetchHack.* Off.

HulkGulp. I fucken will don't mind if I do. Stinks worse
than the trailer. Which is where Ima headed.

HulkShake. Go on. *HandKnee headDangle.*

Whattya been eatin?

HeadShake. Fuck off.

Effen good idea. *StrideWalk.*

HookerTrailer.
GirlSqueak.

MonsterGrowl.
ThinWall poundSound.
FoulTaste vomitHulk staggerStomp.
GreaseCouch leafPorn monsterSprawl.
You in line? *RackHack.*
Naw. There's just skanks tonight.
They're always just skanks.
Not like these. *ThrowMag.* I told that retard I want Asian
chicks. He brought back a carloada fucken Indians!
Fuck you mean all of em?
All of em or most of em.
I told im to start lookin in better spots.
These are all outta the downtown east sleazepit.
Fucken Friendly. What a fucken loser.
You gotta hold yer nose to fuck these hosebags.
There better be at least one white bitch.
Good luck.
Fuck.
You got another onea those onya?
Uh. *SqueezeLeather.* Yeah. Here.
CanToss.
Ah fuck that's. *Kaspoit!* Fucken nice of ya.
DoorFling hulkLurch.
ZipUp.
Geeksterboy. That was quick.
Whoa. *WideLook.* You must really wanna fuck. Last I saw
you were barfin out a week's beer.
It was that fucken dope. Ripped my guts out.
Seemed good to me.
Well thank fuck it went away as quick as it came on.
Yeah you look okay now.
Speaking of which. *SwillGulp.* How's the ho's tonight?
Okay. I got the white one.
Fucken eh. What's with this rezsister fixation of Friendly's?
Donno. Not much difference anyway.

There's a difference.

You got any morea those? *BeerPoint.*

Naw fuck I gave my last one ta this guy here.

Well I better go get me some then. *TotterHulk.* Your turn.

Naw this guy is next.

Fuck it. *ShrugMonster.* You go. I wanna enjoy this fine beverage.

Whatever the fuck my man. *HulkStride.*

AjarDoor. BruiseKnee hardFemme. You next?

Maybe. I seen you before?

HeadShake. Fucked if I know. *DownLook smirkMirth.* Ha ha. *HulkSniff.* Had a shower lately?

Could do with one.

Then do one. And cut the fucked up humour. We'll do the laughin.

ShrugSigh. FumblePurse.

LivingRoom hulkSit.

SkinBook leafBrowse. HallShadow leatherHulk totterStumble zipCrotch.

Fuck.

Yeah. *BoredHulk throwBook.* Fuck.

Yeah fuck. *HulkGrin doorFling downClump stairSteel.*

BeerFridge. Kaspoit! SwillGulp.

Just a sec okay? *DampFemme hallCall.*

DeepSwill.

CanDrop.

HulkRise hallStride.

Just a sec. *HairComb.* Okay?

HulkGrunt unFly. FullCock ableHard.

Just a sec okay.

TwoFinger waistBand lowMove.

BurgeonThrob.

Okay.

PulseGrapple gripWhirl. StiffStare truncheonThrob.

BendOver.

TweenThigh targetSlash.
CockStab.
DryStop.
CockPull. SpitFinger lipCleave. SlipDick fingerGuide.
WetLoose runWork.
DrawBack. RamHit.
RamHit.
WetSlam. FullOn slamGrip. RockFull longStroke ramSlam.
HulkBladder squeezePain. Aw fuck.
Whassamatter?
Shoulda taken a piss.
RamHit. SlamHit. RamHit. SlamHit.
HallNoise swingDoor. KickClose.
SlamHit.
BangSound.
HookerHead wallPound. FaceDown pushUp ramPose.
KnockHead.
KnockHead.
Hey get your hands up and quit that fucken noise eh.
Uh.
PullOut.
DickSheen nearPop.
InSlam.
RamHit.
RamHit ramDick ramHit.
OutStroke. InStroke.
WetHeat.
CoolOut.
HotIn.
CoolHeat airWet.
Ow. Fuck!
PainBlast cumLoad.
Uh. *HulkGrunt.* Fuck.
ComeRam.
PulseJolt.

CoolAir pulseJolt.
LastRam.
Ahhh.
You dick. My head.
StunHulk. DickHold. Ah fuck hold still! *PulseJolt.*
Fuck you.
DickStuck gripHole. PainBack. CockAche.
SlipSlide unHook.
SlowOut teethGrit.
For fuck sakes. *SwabCloth handGrapple.* Next time for fuck-sake gimme a chance to get set. You banged up my face.
Shut the fuck up.
Fuck you.
Worst fuck I've had in years.
Quit trying to cheer me up.
You should pay me.
I'll send you a bill for the band-aid. Cut my forehead.
You're fucken lucky I don't cut ya more.
SeetheFemme crotchWipe.
GutSpasm nauseaBound.
DickSwing hallStagger.
WashRoom standWaver sickPass.
DickPlug multiStream pissSpray.
ShakeDry.
CleansePiss.
CockOver sinkDrain.
SoakSoap rinseJerk. TowelSqueeze.
JeanPack zipUp.
HardSigh.
MirrorDim shadowStubble. JawLine rageVisage.
CloseGlint.
NauseaJolt. GutGird.
SickPass.
GrimaceSmile.
CumDrain crotchEase.

HallTrudge.
HulkLurch.
You next huh.
Yup.
Fuck man.
Yeah I'm gonna fuck man.
Ha ha. *HeadNod.* Go ahead. She's not too bad.
Good.
Maker wash off though.
Yeah?
Fucken stinks for some reason.

SideFire hulkFest.
Kaspoit!
HulkShiver. HalfCan drainBack.
DarkEdge yuckLaugh.
HyperDrunk femmeGiggle.
HulkDaze fireStare.
TalkDrone.
GaggleCry.
CanFling sizzleFlame. WearyDrunk stumbleTrek.
Hey Gort. *CavorterCall.* Want some?
PauseStop.
SoddenDark paperBoard sexPad.
SplayLeg redGash.
Naw Scroaty. I'm hittin it.
Pussy.
Yeah. Pussy. You should see the skank I just fucked. I should
get a fuckmedal for that one man. Effen heroic. Bitches get
fouler by the fucken day.
Hey. *HulkShrug handSplay.* Look where you are.
We're at a pig farm.
Yeah. A pig farm.
SideLook. Sumpms wacky about you right now.
Huh?

You don't always wave around like that when you're standin still.

Huh.

You been doin E?

Zatwhatthatwas? *BackWhirl*. Was that what what was?

RapeGang headTurn.What?

What did you guys feed Scroaty? He looks like a mental bullfrog.

ZipMonster smirkToss. He always looks like a mental bullfrog.

Like a fucked up mental bullfrog. Was it E?

I donno. Hey Scroat. Didya smoke summa that weed?

Huh?

You guys got shit goin in the weed?

Yeah somebody brought some ramped up shit.

Does it make you barf like a dyin dog?

That's the stuff. It did me anyway. Bummer.

I'll fucken say.

We got some left. Wanna?

Naw fuck I barfed enough for one night.

Wanna fuck this bitch? She's still awake.

I've fucken had it. Goin home.

Okay Gort.

Take carea Scroaty willya?

Oh yeah. Whattza matter with im?

He smoked that effen dope.

What effen dope?

HulkSigh.

HulkWalk stiffProng.
YardBarn parkLot.
GleamRow.
ElectroKey VetteWake.
TrunkOpen.
LeatherOff. MudShit bootScrape. SlipOn stepIn.
TrunkRummage. LaundroClean bowlShirt. QuickChange.

DoorOpen.
SeatRecline.
HairComb.
MotorPurr lightsOn seatBelt reverseGear clutchDrop.
FirstGear weaveCourse slalomSteer.
LeanPark cycleSchool.
MercedesSport uteTruck.
CaddySport uteTruck.
PorscheSport uteTruck.
HummerHulk.
RaceWagon.
ShagVan.
HookerJitney.
PigBarn wreckYard trailerMorgue.
ShedSpread machineDump.
RutPath.
ClearBerm roadRange.
BlackTop ChevPurr.
CruiseJoy.
JoltSnap. RearView copSight.
RedLight sideStop.
SideGlance eyeCheck.
HandWave.
CopCheck.
HandWave.
CruiserBlink speedTurn.
SighMonster.
SpeedLane.

Morning; bedroom: Moanrack

LightStab painBlaze.
Wake the fuck up! I need some parenting help here.
SleepHulk dreamWet stunDrool. Wha?
That damn kidda yours.
Huh?
Reinhart's being a fuckhead again.
EyeBlink. What fucken time is it?
Time for the little prick to go to school but he won't get out
of bed.
Tell him. *HulkRoll.* I'll kick his fucken head in if he's not
out of here in five minutes. *EyeClose.*
I'm not his mom.
Snore.
Don't you go back to fucking sleep.
Pretty fucken hard to do under the circumstances.
Go talk to him.
Why?
He won't listen to me.
Talk louder.
He says I'm not his mom so what I say is shit.
HulkSigh. Issat what he's sayin? *OpenEye.*
What do you think?
RollSit. Hand me a paira gaunch. *YawnStretch.*
FlyLaundry.
HallTrek stumbleWalk.
Hey.
Whaddya want?
Open the fucken door.
Fuck you.

I'm only gonna say once.

Then you're gonna shit a brick. Right?

HeadShake.

BackStep. FootAim.

BareHeel doorCrash.

HollowBoom swingSlam wallBounce.

Nice going Dad.

What did Linda just tell you to do?

That bitch.

What did that bitch tell you to do?

Go to school.

Why aren't you doin it?

I got too fucken wrecked last night.

Get the fuck up and go to school.

My head hurts.

It'll hurt a lot more when I kick it.

You wouldn't fucken dare.

You wanna find out?

They told us at school. I could have you charged with assault.

SighPause. Lookit punk.

Don't call me that.

I'll callya whateverthefuck I wanna callya but that's not what I wanna talk about right now.

Oh you wanna talk?

Yeah.

What about?

I donno. Is there any point?

Point to what?

Look I hope it's not too obvious. You fucken need a lesson.

I go to school for that.

You know what I'm talkin about. Is now the time?

Fuck you.

All of fifteen fucken years old and fulla piss. *WaverGrin.* Reminds me of me.

Ain't that fucken sweet.

Okay. You called it kid. Just remember.
What?
Just remember. Yer gonna get a fine shitkickin from yer old man. Pretty major turnpoint. Just like my old man did for me. Everything changed after that. Twenty-some years ago.
Spare me the hokey shit and leave me alone.
Look what you got. Money. House. Fucken cars to be chauffeured around in.
So what?
Just to give fair warning. *ThroatRasp clearHack.* Because you are my son. I'm going to give you a major lickin if you do not rise from that bed right now and get your skuzzy bunghole to school. *Comprende?*
KidGlare.
Don't be usin yer pissy look on me. Maybe it works on the little kids at school but it won't do you any fucken good around here.
ShrugSneer.
HulkStride scruffGrip.
Hey.
Shut up. *HeadSlap.*
Hey!
SlapHand backSlap whipSlap.
Fuck!
CuffSlap. What's with all the talk? *ScalpCuff.* You're being bitchslapped. *ScruffShake.* Whattyou. *FaceWhack.* Gonna do about it?
LimberWind faceWhack.
KidScramble.
LimbFling.
CloseFist twoHit.
KidFling offBed.
GutKick.
Get up.
KidCough.

Get up!
DoubleCough bendKnee.
Get the fuck up.
LeerGlare slowRise.
EarPunch.
KidStagger handFlay.
Don't just wave at me like a faggot! *BackStand.* You're bein punched. What do you do?
EyeRed boxMove.
ParryShift elbowJab.
BackStand.
KidMouth wipeStare.
Come on.
KidQuick shoulderDrive hardBash.
StumbleHulk. Not bad!
ArmHold neckChoke uniStumble.
WallCrash.
KidFace wallMash.
NeckWrench stumbleWalk mirrorView.
See that?
PurpleFace.
See that?
Uhhhhhh!
See that?
What!
That there's an asshole with a big mouth and no balls.
StruggleGasp.
KidGrapple.
Relax. If I wanted you to go down you'd be going down.
HoldLoose sputterFall.
Any more need to talk?
CoughHack.
Now get your sad ass to school.
HulkTurn stumbleWalk.
MegaSigh.

Toilet Room piss Stop. Arc Run. Mega Sigh.
Water Run face Wash.
Crotch Firm.
Gaunch Pull. Soap Stroke. Hand Stroke hand Stroke.
Jerk Image open Splay hooker Bend.
Cunt cunt cunt.
Jack Pop.
Cunt cunt cunt!
Milk Through cleanse Pull.
Yellow Tone pump Spray.
Pump Milk white Pump.
Dribble Drip white Pulse.
Slouch Lean hulk Sigh prong Flag.
Ease Breath.
Hall Stride.
Where you been?
Had to shitkick my kid. Then wash my fucken face.
Femme Stand arm Fold.
What's yer fucken problem?
You were supposed to talk to him not beat him up.
You tellin me how to parent?
You're just as fucked up as he is.
I wanna go back to sleep.
What a couple of fucking assholes.
Aw shut up.
I will not shut up until there's some sanity in this house.
Sanity's fucken overrated.
How would you know? That fucking kid of yours is crazy
enough for all three of us.
Just you never mind. And where the fuck you get off talking
to my son like that?
Somebody's got to tell him to at least go to school.
Nobody tells him nothin except me. If we got crazy shit I'll
deal with the crazy shit. If we got teen rebellion I'll deal with
the fucken teen rebellion.

By way of violence?
Liked that eh?
You're an effing maniac.
Just doin what needs to be done.
Are you kidding? They'll throw you in jail.
Not if nobody knows.
He'll go squealing as soon as he gets to school.
You don't know that kid. You don't know this family.
What are you talking about? This isn't a family. One maniac
and one girlfriend and one psycho kid do not make a family.
Whateverthefuck.
That kind of attitude will get you busted for sure.
Just fucken relax willya?
What about the bruises?
He fell down some stairs.
As if.
That's what he'll tell them. If they ask.
We'll see.
You'll see.
Either way. One fucked up kid.
I'm proud of him.
What?
All through that beating. Not a peep.
What?
No whinin. No tears. He's a good kid.
That is screwed up. I can't even begin.
I'll screw you up.
HandSnatch femmeWear.
Oh no fucken way! *FemmeFlee.*
No fucken way what? *HulkChase.*
No fucken way you're going to fuck me. *BedJump.*
Nowhere to run. *AnkleGrip.* Bitch. Ooooh.
LungeGrab.
PantyRip.
NimbleNude wrestleFlop.

Here it is babe.
Ooooh.
HandCrotch rubGrip.
CrawlOn breastLick.
CockTip crackSearch.
FingerDown lipSpread.
Ooooh.
There's my cunt.
Yes.
You're my cunt.
StabReady cockTip.
FrictoRub.
Ooooh.
Wet cunt.
My wet cunt.
Fuck me.
My cunt.
Why aren't you hard?
I'm hard.
Not hard enough.
Gimme a sec.
Fuck you.
Come on baby.
FemmeWriggle upSit. Have you been fucking whores?
Oh fuck off.
If you fucked a whore I want you to jerk off.
I just did.
When?
When I washed up.
Just now?
Yeah.
No wonder you're not so hard.
I'm always hard for you baby.
Well okay. But I don't want you sticking that thing in me
and squirting all kinds of yellow hooker juice.

I shot it all off.
You better.
I tellya I did. Honest.
You better always jerk off before you come in me.
I just jerked off okay?
Did it come out yellow?
At first. Then white.
It fucken better.
I'm gettin hard.
Are you?
Uh huh.
How come?
All this fucktalk.
Oh. *ProngFondle*. You are.
Uh huh.
Oh. Me too.
Gettin wet?
Oh fuck. *BackSpread*. Stick me.
Don't have to ask me twice baby. Huh!
Oooh.
ShortBreath. Cunt.
Cunt.
Cunt.
Cunt.
Oooh.
NoBreath strokePlunge.
SatinSlide slipVelvet.
Oooh.
HardRam. Ah ah ah ah. *RamSlam*.
My asshole fuck machine.
My cunt. *RamSlam*. My perfect cunt. Fightin and fuckin and fucken fightin and fucken fucking.
Asshole.
Cunt. *IdlePause*. I'm fucking you.
You're fucking me.

I'm fucking you. *DickStrive.*
LegSplay tenseTunnel.
Ah.
VagiPress.
Ah!
VagiFlex.
Ahhhhh! *CockLost ejaculoSuction.*
SweetFrictive cumExtract.
LostHulk.
InterioTight vagiFlex.
Ah!
SeminaBlast. PulseBlow.
SlamShot cumLoad.
VagiFlex.
Oooh. Stop it baby.
No!
Oh. Pain. Still shootin. What a load.
My my.
Oh yeah.
Good come there baby.
Oh yeah. For you.
Yeah for me.
You do it. Every time.
Anytime for you baby.
UniClasp.
Oh man. *ShrivelPull oozeOut.* I think I came a gallon.
You're pouring out of me.
Yeah. *PalmWide vagiHold.* Lotsa me in there all right. *Slip-Swish vagiRub.*
Oooh.
SwishFinger clitStroke.
Oooh Oooh. Yeah.
SquishMassage. WideStroke.
Eiiii! *VagiTwitch.*
There you go baby.

Oh.
Uh huh.
UniBreathe.
HallThump.
Reinhart!
StartQuiet.
Are you fucken listenin out there?
He's done it before.
HulkRise. He fucken better not.
He as much as told me.
PantGrab. Fucken perv. *FlingDoor.*
BackPack schoolReady. I need cash.
How long you been standin here?
I haven't.
Liar.
Fuck it Dad. I'm not lyin. You want me to go to school or
not?
PocketFumble pantSearch. Here. *WalletFifty pullProffer.*
Okay.
And quit spyin on me an Linda.
Okay okay. *KidExit.*
HulkAbed.
You are the fuckenest weirdo.
BlearEye. Surprised?
Fifty bucks.
Kid may not be a wheel around here. But he is at school.
Glad I don't have a kid at school. What fucked up values.
You got other things that're fucked up.
Fuck you.
If I hadn't just fucked you I'd give you a good shitkickin too.
Lay a hand on me and I'll fucking shoot you.
Ah baby. You know what turns me on.
FemmeSmile. Guess so.
You know me.
I know you.

I just fucked you.
You fucked me good.
Well then. *HeadSink.* Shut the fuck up then. And let's get
some sleep.
ShoulderShake.
You better get up.
EyeBlear. Why?
Didn't you hear the phone?
Fuck no. Who was it?
Roberto.
Oh.   .
You have to meet him.
I do huh?
At three.
What time is it now?
Almost one.
Fuck.
At the place.
Okay. *ClockPeer.* Fuck.
FemmeDelta straddleCrotch. What do you want for breakfast?
HulkGroan. Not that.

Afternoon; compound: SitDown

WhirrMotor gateRise.
VetteCar parkStop.
MetalDoor buzzOpen.
CoolDark poolHall.
SullenHulk nestleSpot.
BarMonster eyeScreen.
BelowBar handReach.
MetalDoor buzzOpen.
Zat you Gort? *ElectroVoice.*
Roberto.
DoorBuzz.
Gortboy! *BowlShirt tanHulk.* Howareya?
Can't complain.
Nobody'd.
Listen if I.
Did.
Right. You got it.
Sorry to get you going so early.
Whatever.
Sit yerself down.
Don't. *FlumpLeather wingBack.* Mind if I do.
Got a helluva lotta stuff on the go.
Okay.
Gotta have a jaw with ya first.
Oh?
Yeah. Want a drink?
What's that you got?
Scotch.
I'll have some.

Good man.

BoozePour. GlassPass.

HulkSlug. Oh man. This is strong shit for this early.

Put hair on your ass.

Huh.

FlumpLeather wingBack. Now then.

Yeah.

Friendly's eh?

Oh yeah?

Yup.

Uh huh.

We been okay with your job so far.

Good.

But there's complaints right?

Oh?

Late hookers. Too few too skank. Beer shortage. Fucken filth.

It's a pig farm.

Everybody knows that.

Good. Then what?

Then last night the power went out in the hooker trailer.

I was there. I didn't see it.

Well it happened. About the time the bitch turned up dead.

What?

The dead bitch.

What dead bitch?

You didn't know?

No.

Some broad croaked.

When?

Oh fuck I don't know. Just heard about it. Sometime early morning I'd guess. That's the kind of detail I expect you to know.

Why the fuck didn't somebody tell me?

That's just it pardner. *SwillGlass.* How close you keeping

this family of fuckers you got running the place?

Pretty close. I saw em last night.

Saw them yeah. Saw them. That's it though. No?

Whatyou tryina say?

Why didn't you know about the stiff hooker?

Nobody told me.

Or the electric fuckup?

Nobody told me about that either.

Who at the farm would tell you?

Friendly.

Okay. Why do you think he didn't?

I don't know.

Why don't you know?

Fuck.

Gort. We like you around here. You know that. And back east they like what we like. Papajohn thinks you're the tops. He told me himself. He might even get off his froggy ass and get out here some day soon. Imagine that.

So they think we're doin okay.

They think we got a paradise out here. That's all there is to it.

From what I hear they got things pretty good too.

Oh I hear stuff either way. The important thing is here.

So we're doin fine here?

Right you are. No worries. But considering how important that is. How vital to the overall operation. Gort baby. I get a slight feeling you don't take your calling with us all that seriously.

Doin the best I can.

I want to believe that.

Okay.

Look. I need you to know this. Our operations here. *EyeNàrrow.* Despite appearances. It isn't just a lot of drinking and fucking. Hyuck yuck. Although admittedly it does involve a lot of drinking and fucking. Hyuck yuck. But what I'm saying is it's not all drinking and fucking.

I know that.

Do you? Go over your last day and a half for me.

What?

Your movements. So to speak. What you've been up to.

I was at the boozecan last night.

Of course. And Friendly was there?

And his sister that skank and his brother Stew.

Yeah that guy. Is his real name Stuart?

Fucked if I know. We call him Stew because he keeps a pot of beefdip back of the bar.

Uh huh. *SwillGlass*. What's the sister's name?

I can't fucken remember.

Wouldn't it be your business to remember?

I don't know if I ever knew.

What does she do?

Keeps the books.

Important job. No?

I guess.

And you don't know her name.

Karen or Sandra or something.

Is that a good way to run a business?

Place is a shithouse anyway. Always was.

It's a shithouse because we need it to be a shithouse. Or at least look damn like a shithouse. Keeps the straightjohn citizens away. Keeps the cops away.

Okay then. So nobody should complain about the mess.

We expect mess out by the fire. Off in the pasture. But away from the parking lot. And especially the buildings. Especially the hooker building. But word is there's bugs in the bedding. The hooker trailer is crawling from what I understand. And the bar isn't kept clean and well stocked. What do you say to that?

Maybe. I'm workin on it.

See that you do.

RoomTick.

LeatherSqueak.
Is that what was on your mind?
BangDistant poolPlay breakShot.
How's it going with the Ruckmumps?
Fine I guess.
You guess. Ever see em?
Saw one last night. Constable Paquette I'm pretty sure.
After midnight?
Uh huh.
Darkish late twenty-something? Heavy liphair?
Yeah.
Must have been him.
I seen him once before.
Where last night?
Outside. As I was driving away. Followed me a while.
No trouble?
None. Just freaky for a bit.
Did he give you a wave?
He gave me a wave.
Good boy. Paquette's my personal bumboy. Raised him
from a pup.
Fucken eh. Nice job.
Not hard. They recruit heavily in Quebec. Then send the
poor buggers out here. All he wants is to get back to *La Belle
Province* and he'll do considerable toward that objective.
Royal Canadian Mountfuck Police.
Watch your mouth. The Ruckmumps are our best friends.
Worst copforce in the world.
Effen eh worst copforce in the world and that's the safest
mealticket we can get.
Buncha nerds.
Bunch of eager rural nerds. Excommunicated to isolated
dives as far from their homes as possible. Suspicious of every-
body. Blind to friends. Scared of enemies. These are just the
paranoid fuckers we need if we need any at all sniffing around

our shit. I say again. These are just the guys to be investigating quote unquote our so-called affairs. Et cetera. They are to be fed and watered daily. Get me?

I understand the strategy.

Good boy. We need cops. We need people obeying the rules. Without people obeying the rules there's no percentage in being an outlaw. Everybody's growing their own dope stealing their own cars fucking their own women we don't make any money. So we treat the cops fair. Throw them the occasional tasty treat. They throw us a whole bunch back. We pretend to be friendly with them. They pretend to be friendly with us. Works good.

No argument.

And speaking of strategy. How's the moving company going?

Fine.

Any personnel concerns?

Nope. Pipeline to the federal joints is still open. We get em as soon as they're released. Badass ironpumping excons. Natural swampers.

Good to hear. And the alarm outfit?

Profitable as usual.

A fine business model there.

You think so?

When I heard it I thought. There's genius.

Pretty simple if you ask me.

The best ones always are.

If you say so.

Well come on bro. You're not hurting.

I had some heat from the valley Ruckmumps. Twice they caught the same guys fencing and one of em works for me.

Now that's just sloppy. You advertise?

In all the talk radio markets.

Okay. You know the set up.

Sure I do.

Let's go over it again.

Why.

Just so's I know you know.

If we gotta.

We gotta. Okay. You case houses.

Sometimes they buy sometimes they don't.

Doesn't matter. All the goods are inventoried.

Diagrams of the layouts handed off to outoftowners. I never completely understood that part.

Your guys take a vacation and go service one of my areas or even across the country. My guys come to you. Cops pinch one crew they bugger off on bail and never see them again for a good long time if ever. Makes for better business all round.

Okay I get it.

We been doing that. Right?

Right.

It's the procedure. Right?

Right.

Then how can it screw up? What about this clown of yours they caught?

Jeeze Roberto think about it. Guys get greedy. You can't stop em from freelancing. Specially if they see somethin sweet.

That's where the baseball bats come in.

Yeah it sounds easy. But what if it's your old lady's little brother?

Then you lose a brother-in-law.

And I get little or no fucking.

You get fucking from every which direction.

Not like my ol lady.

SmileWide. She's a dancer right?

You seen her.

Fucken hot. Nice goen there Gort.

Thanks Roberto.

But irregardless. Whoeverthefuck's brother he is. Anybody stupid enough to draw heat from the cops you get rid of the dickhead. Right?

If you say so.
You know I do.
I know you do.
Good then. *HeadNod swillGlass.* You up to date?
You mean dues?
What the fuck else would I mean?
Yeah. Put a big wad in last week.
I saw. Well done.
Business is good. I keep tellin ya.
That's why you're still drinking and fucking my friend.
SwillGlass. HulkSmirk.
Hah!
Heh heh.
Hah hah hah. *KneeSlap.*
So.
So bro. You know what you gotta do.
I know what I gotta do.
By the way. How's Scroaty?
Scuzzy as usual.
He better lay low.
Why?
Oh some business needs doing.
Should I know?
Probably. We're calling in a couple of bodies from back east.
Bodies?
Uh huh. Workmen. In fact. Might need to get you to put em up.
The usual?
Yeah. Nothing fancy.
Fine. There's room at the farm. *SwillBooze.* Can I ask what's the deal?
Might as well. It'll likely involve you before it's all done.
Yeah?
Scroaty fucked up grand. You know those two shitrats he's got?

His mule corps? Jerry and Shirt.

I think that's their fucken names. They got pissed in some Bellingham dive last week.

I think I heard. What's unusual?

They'd just run a load down. Had the cash. And the blow. Got drinking. Got in a fight. Ended up in city lockup. Scroaty had to go down and drive the fucken minivan back.

The cops got the money and the blow?

Fuck no. The kids at least put the stuff in a safe place. Scroat did what he had to do. Got a box in a safe deposit and laid it all aside. Cleaned up the van. No. That part was fine. But when he drove through the border the sniffer dog checked his ride and found a stash of blow inside a pillow in the back seat.

Yer shittin me.

I fucken wish.

Those effin cunts.

You're not kidding.

Whatter we gonna do with em?

Nevermind that for now. I got these guys coming out. To handle things. There's even more to it but nevermind. They'll clean up the Scroaty situation.

Okay.

You want details?

Do I hafta?

No.

Then I doen wanna.

Good boy.

Strictly need to know.

That's the rule.

I'm stickin with it.

Just as well.

Okay. *TossBack cleanGlass.* If that's the total scoop. I'll get going.

Get going.

Gotta see about this dead fucken hooker.

You know it.

Damn it anyway. *HulkRise.*

Hold back a sec. Your movements.

What?

At the boozecan last night. Any fights?

One.

Good?

Not bad. I plowed Geeksterman.

Hah! That fucker.

No kiddin.

Then what?

I dunno. The fire.

Gangfuck?

Of course.

Was she holding together by the time you got in?

Didn't bother. Got it off with a trailercunt.

Outstanding. Was she reasonably clean?

I made her shower.

Good policy. So after the boozecan. You drove home?

Yeah.

Fuck the old lady?

Nunna yer bizness.

Hah hah!

Dirty old fucker.

How's your boy?

Fine.

Whatsis name again?

Reinhart.

AKA The Damned.

Livin up to his nickname.

He'll be a wonder in a few years.

Fuck the few years. I had to shitkick him this very fucken day.

No kidding. What was the issue?

Not going to school. Lippin off his stepmother.

Hey if it's nothing more serious than that you got no problems.

Had to go to a school meeting last week. Fucken kid is the school's worst bully.

Yeah?

Apparently shitkicked some faggy kid over nothing. Then grabbed some hot little bitch by the snatch.

Teacher?

Student.

Hmmm. *DarkFace.* The bully stuff is fine. Builds immunity. But skinner shit we don't need.

Don't think he knew what he was doin.

How old again?

Fifteen.

Oh he knows what he's doing all right. Better keep a clamp on that.

Yeah.

Last thing we need is a fucking skinner kid coming up in the mix. Stealing. Shitkicking. Dealing. Racing cars. That's all cool. But sex beefs are what the media likes to dance around on. Let them dance around on some other socioethnic community subset like the Hindus or the Mormons or the Muslims or the Moose Lodge or somesuch other kind of bullshit turban outfit and stay the fuck away from us. That means no twisted sisters in the camp. No? That means any kind of kinkoid crap gets dealt with pronto. Understood?

I don't think the Mormons wear turbans.

Whateverthefuck. You get me huh?

Fucken eh.

I gotta get onto other stuff.

Right.

I want to report all good back east.

You can.

I can.

At least from my end.
See to it.
I'm goin there right now.

Late afternoon; SUV: DogRoll

OneHand hulkDrive.
StabDial.
RingTone.
You have reached the voicemailbox for.
ReStab. RingTone toneTone.
Fuck! *CrossVette angerThrow.*
DriveSwerve boozeCan roadEnter.
BrownBlack lowBlur.
YelpStrike.
ScreechPark.
HulkLeap.
ScurryFemme.
You seen Sidewinder?
What?
My dog.
You mean the piecea shit I just ran over tryin to drive in here?
FretShriek dashAway.
HulkStep smellRoute.
Fuck Friendly!
GrimeClad ragWaif.
What the fuck is that fucken smell?
Oh. *RagWhirl.* Gort.
Yeah it's oh Gort all right. What the fuck is goin on?
Whattya mean?
First of all. You got a fucken morgue in there?
Where?
That shithouse workshopa yours.
Oh the smell?
Whatthefuckya think I'm talkin about?
Manure on my veggie patch.

Huh?

Out back. My garden. Yeah. Doesn't bother me. I kinda get used to it.

I never want to get used to it. What is it. Dogshit?

Pig manure. From our last remainin pig. Nothin better.

Opinion Friendly. Opinion. How long you had a garden?

This happens to be a ackshual farm Gort.

All I know is five years ago you and your brother and sister were cryin to us cause you couldn't pay the taxes cause the city said you weren't usin it enough for a farm and they wanted to build houses on it.

Yeah yeah.

Yeah so we run it as something other than a farm and we pay the taxes. Happy happy. Now you say the place is back to bein a farm.

Yeah.

By name only. For appearance only. It's not sposed to be an actual farm.

I just got a little garden.

With pigshit on it. Smells like a fucken livestock pen around here.

Yeah yeah.

Yeah yeah. So dig this shitfield up and pave it over.

I never didn't have a veggie patch.

Get fucken rid of it. Hear me?

Okay okay. *FrownWaif.* Ya just come over here in the middle of the day to tell me that or do you wanna talk about somethin important?

Yeah I do. *HeadNod.* That tin shithousea yours habitable?

You mean can we sit down in it?

What the fuck you think I mean?

Well sure we can sit down in it.

DuoStride innerDark.

Man. *HulkBreath.* Thank fuck it doesn't smell so bad in here.

Yeah. I just spread it on this mornin. It'll ease off in a couplea days.

Well don't let it foul the air all the way over to the hooker unit.

Oh the breeze'll keep it away by tonight. Always does.

You're sure about that.

Yup.

How can you be so sure about somethin like the breeze?

Lived here all my life. Can set my watch if I had one by the hour the evenin heat eases back and lets the cool off the mountains slide down. Same for the mornin heatup that sucks in the west air so far sometimes you can smell the sea.

EyeRoll. Fucken fascinating.

Anythin else you'd care to know bout the weather round here Gort?

Don't get smart.

That's somethin nobody ever cused me of.

I can imagine.

WoodTin doorSlam.

SobAngry stickWield weepWoman. LimpLoose pitPup.

What? *StartleHulk.* The fuck!

Aw no. *SadRagged.* What happened to Sidewinder?

This fuckhead killed him. *DogThrow.*

SideStep corpseDodge. Fuck you.

DogBody floorClunk.

StickDraw. Don't you know how to fucken drive!

Keep your fucken dead dog to yourself you ugly skank. And put that club down if you wanna live til lunchtime. Now get the fuck outta here. I gotta do business with your halfwit brother.

KneelRagged. Aw Sidewinder. *StrokeFur.*

For fucksakes.

He was our dog.

Get another one. *PantPocket digSearch.* Here's twenty bucks. Go to the pound and pick out somethin even uglier. And keep yer livestock off the fucken road. What the fuck was he doin in the driveway anyways? I should call the SPC fucken A on you dimwits.

Yeah you'd rat out real quick wouldn't ya faggot! *WeepAnger*.

I'm fucken kiddin you whore reject you. Keep your fucken slagmouth to yourself. Now do as I say and go the fuck away so Friendly an me can talk without gaggin at your disgusting smell. Comprende?

BackStep.You'll get yours dickweed. You just wait. *BackStep*. *RaggedStoop softSob*.

Tell that skankwitch she better watch out who she threatens around here.

It's her own place. *RedEye upLook*. Just like mine. *SniffSob*. He was just a pup.

Lookit. Do I always have to be the one who tries to convince you three that you don't have a so-called own place anymore?

No you don't. *UpStand eyeWipe*. You just have to tell me what it is you come here for and get the heck away afterward.

Now don't you get started on the road to a shitkickin too. We can't have all your crew laid up. I came here to giveya royal shit for the way you're runnin this place.

Me? Runnin this place? I thought you were.

Lookit dickhead. You got a simple job. Keep the place reasonably clean. Turn on the lights in the bar. Keep booze in the fridge. Cut firewood for the fire. Collect the hookers for the night's entertainment. What's hard about anya this?

Nothin. I been doin it.

No you haven't. The place is a shitpalace. The bar's got an incha dirt on the floor. The hooker unit bathrooms look like backalley dumpsters. Half the booze in the bar hasn't been re-stocked for weeks. The wood for the fire is so wet it barely fucken burns. And last night you were so late with the hookers half the guys left.

Oh yeah. One of em's dead.

And that's another fucken thing. Why didn't I hear about it

from you? Pretty damn quick. Why werentcha on the fucken phone to me first thing?

Whattya mean? *SoftLift deadDog.*

I mean you got clear instructions to call me if anything around here happens.

DoorWard corpseBear. I didn't know that.

The fuck you didn't. Where you goin?

To bury Sidewinder. Less you want me ta let him sit around here and start stinkin.

Where's this dead hooker?

Come on.

DuoTrek dirtWalk.

ToolStop shovelGrip.

I wanna see this hooker. Forget about yer stupid dog.

This is the way Gort. Or doncha know where the hooker trailer is?

Isn't she out by the firepit? Did somebody move her?

Whattya talkin about?

The gangfuck bitch. Isn't that the one?

Naw. She left with the rest of em this mornin. Won't be back soon though I'll tell ya. Poor thing. Whinin away.

HookerHome stairDoor.

WindowSun stabHarsh.

DeadProne femmeStiff.

Holy crap. *SquintHulk.* This is the bitch I fucked last night.

And umpteen other guys.

Who found her?

Nobody found her. Scroaty was doin er and she croaked. That's what he said.

Scroaty?

Yeah. See that carrot out er bottom?

Yeah.

Somethin to do with the Scroaty method. Parently.

Oh yeah. Small dick.

Whatever you say Gort.

No it's fucken true apparently. He puts a carrot up there to crowd things up. Never tried it m'self but I guess it might work.

All kindsa stoopidity if you ask me.

And hard on the plumbing. You gotta pay em extra for it.

But that don't look like what kilter.

Oh hell no of course not. *HardLook handTouch.* Ugh. She's fucken stiff.

That's what happens.

Looks like she was frothing at the mouth.

Straight druggy stuff eh?

Issat barf?

Round er mouth?

On the pillow there. And down here on the floor.

Kinda looks like it.

Huh. Musta been sick to begin with or somethin.

Or took something that didn't agree with er.

Uh. I smoked some weed last night that made my guts feel like packin up and shippin out.

Maybe that got er.

Naw. Tough broad like this.

Sometimes tough don't cut it Gort.

Whattyou? A philosopher now?

Just sayin.

Well. Whateverthefuck. We gotta act fast here.

All right. Okay. So what now?

Whaddya mean what now?

Whadda we do with er?

Well for one thing no fucken way we call the cops.

I figgered that.

And we can't dump er. I gotta think here. That'd be pointin an arrow straight at this place.

Uh huh.

Where exactly did you get er?

This one? *FurrowBrow.* Um. Maybe on Hastings. At Princess.

Were there lots?

Lottsa what?

Other hookers stupid.

Oh halfadozen.

Anya them come along?

Not that bunch. She was the only one wanted to come. T'others were gettin all p'ticalar. That's why I had to drive around so long.

Well okay. Nobody else from that corner?

Nope.

Good. Just bury er. They'll all think she left town.

Bury er?

Yeah. You got that shovel in yer hand. You got the big empty lot out back. Make a big enough hole and throw er in there with yer dog.

Well. Not with Sidewinder. But okay I guess.

First of all take off the rest of er clothes. Grab er bag there. *HandRifle*. Here's eighty bucks.

ProfferReach. Take half.

ShovelDrop. *DogDrop*.

WaifStash cashPocket.

You want this watch?

I been livin without one forty-six years. *EyePeer wideTimex*. Cute pitjer though. Is that a panda bear?

Take all this stuff and her clothes and burn em. *ToteBag bed-Toss*. Today. ASAP. Put er in the ground someplace I don't know and never tell me where. If anybody calls about er tellem you donno who the fuck they're talkin about. Wear gloves. Wash yer hands after you do it. Wash yer mouth out with soap. We donno who this bitch is and we never fucken wanna know. Then forget about the whole fucken thing. Comprende?

If you say so.

I do say so. And what about that other stuff?

What other stuff?

The filth. The booze. The hooker timetable. I doen want any more complaints.

I'll see what I can do.

You better do better than that.

We need more cash to run this place.

You're gettin plenty now.

We gotta buy a new dog.

What the fuckerya talkin about? Half the guys in this club got rottie and pitbull and canario pups up the ass. You can get all the watchdog meat you need with a note up on the board.

We ain't lookin for a watchdog. We're here all the time anyway. We want a pet.

Fucken place is infested with rats. Make friends with onea them.

Very funny.

Just do yer job.

You like pushin people around dontcha Gort?

Lookit Friendly. *HeadShake shrugSigh.* I know you guys don't like your lives. Sweet fuckall anybody can do about that. But try not to leak your crapulation onto the rest of the world okay? As long as you know your place you'll be fine. I just had to shitkick my own kid to make this point. Do I have to do the same to you?

Don't try it Gort I'm warnin ya.

What has gotten into you guys out here? First your sister now you.

We get tireda all the crap.

It's way late to be gettin tireda anythin and you guys know it. Whatddya think we'd pick up and go someplace else just because you don't like us anymore?

Well runnin the boozecan and choppin firewood is one thing. But gettin ridda bodies. That ain't in the job description.

Your job is anything we say it is dumbass.

No need to go callin a fella names.

I'll call you whatthefuckever I figger you deserve at whatever time I decide you deserve it fuckwad.

DumbWaif.

And another thing. Sumpm like this happens again on this farm and you don't get word to me first and foremost and before anybody else in the whole fucken world and you join this stiff under the pigshit. Got that?

FurrowGrimace.

Answer me.

I got that.

You have my cell number?

Uh huh. Tattooed over my heart.

Fucken good place for it. *BackStep.* Now get this bitch's clothes off and bury her.

Late morning; Trans-Canada Rte. 1: ArmTrade

DuoMonster uteDrive.
Wish we coulda got a beemer or something.
DriveHulk wheelTap. Acuras are good enough.
We deserve class no?
Consider it a Jap Mercedes. Besides we don't want something too good. The mud on this place is sposed to be fierce.
This whole fucken place is fierce. *SideGlare.* Lookit those mountains.
I think that's sposed to be Mount Baker. A volcano.
Volcano? No shit.
It only goes off once in a while's what I understand.
Fucken alpha scungefuck. *HeadShake.* How much we gettin for this again?
Morn we ever got for anyfuckenthing else.
Better be. Havin to go from civilization to the land of volcanos. Gimme MontrealTorontoWindsorDetroit anytime.
Gotta go where the work is.
I guess.
Speaking of which Chico me boy. Get that map out and tell me where to turn.
GloveBox paperGrapple. Which fucken map? British Columbia? Vancouver?
Whichever shows the Fraser Valley.
Huh. They both do but different sizes. Wait a minute.
Hurry up. I think I gotta turn at some kinda lake exit.
What was the name of the place?
Sputzum Flats. Or Sputum River. Retchwater Canyon. Spitup Breakfast. Or somesuch fucken crazy name like that.

There's a place called Spuzzum.

That's it.

What kind of fucken name is that for a town?

It's not even a town from what I heard. And we don't go all the way in there. If there's an in there to go into. We got a turnoff.

Okay. Lemme have a good look at this thing.

He's out in the boonies. Away from everywhere.

He fucken better be.

Effen eh.

There's a road here looks like a dirt track. Dotted line on the map.

That'll be it.

Where are we right now?

Just past a burg called Agasee.

Oh fuck wheressat? Lemme see. No Agasee anywhere here.

I think it's spelled funny. Like a French name.

Fuck me I don't see it. Unless it's this weird one. Aga-sizz. A-gassy. Could that be it?

Likely.

Okay good. If that's the place then we're about a couple inches away.

Left or right?

Right.

Lemme know when.

Looks like you go over a river. Then right.

Gotcha.

Might be another hour or so.

Okay.

SighMonster. Pretty boring.

C'mon. Enjoy the scenery.

Fuck the scenery. I watch Discovery Channel for scenery.

DriverSigh. There's just no pleasing a guy like you Chico.

I'll be pleased we just get there and do our bizness and get the fuck back to something that looks like a city.

Fast as we can.
FreeDistance boredomStretch timeDrag.
DriverHulk yawnLurch.
Hey fuckwad! Don't go off the road.
Fuck me I shoulda slept on the plane.
Want me to drive?
Naw here's the bridge. We're almost there.
Yeah that looks like it.
SylvaScape mountainClimb pitchRoad.
WheelHulk knuckleClutch. It's a fucken four-by adventure.
He has to be remote. The stuff this guy's into.
MultiKilometre trekDrive.
ClearCut vastWood.
FarmPasture openRange.
Look for chainlink fence and some honkin security camera shit.
That's it right there. *FingerPoint.* Nothin else out here.
RollStop.
KeyLock speakerPost.
CrackleStatic.
OverHead cameraShift. SwivelRange.
CrackleStatic. Whoddafuck issat? *CrackleStatic.*
Rudy? Is that you?
CrackleStatic.
You really gotta get some improved electronics man. I can barely hear ya.
DeadSound.
WhirrMotor gateSwing.
Guess he heard ya.
GravelRut slowDrive.
RavineSpan.
VastOpen mudPlain.
TreeGrove clearSpace.
QuonsetMetal jumboHangar.
HangarDoor loneMan. GunHeavy.

ThickBody toughDog barkSnap.
Rudy seems like the nervous type.
Okay I heard the deal is you get out slow with your hands
in sight and step away from the rig.
One at a time. I don't like the looka that piece he's holding.
You first.
DriverDoor slowWide. StepMonster.
PassengerDoor slowWide. OutStep.
GrowlDog sniffClose.
FreezeMonster.
Vell Vhattya know. Chico and Flame. Ride on dime.
Rudy. How are ya?
Ja Chico djust vine.
Been a while.
Ja years. Back east when I vas last. How are tings dere?
Fine.
ThreeWay lookOver.
TeutonHard terrorHound growlSniff.
Mind if we come into your little shop of horrors?
Ja don't move yet. Fritzie! Fritzie!
DogStop.
Kommen sie. *WhineGrowl.* In now!
SniffGrowl heelToe.
LegSniff.
CrotchSniff.
Fritzie!
DogSnuffle offTrot.
Okay. You can valk around now. You pass inspection ja.
StrideMonsters.
GreetShake.
You vant a beer?
Don't fucken mind if we do.
RoughHand sixPack.
You sure take care of security around here Rude. *Kaspoit!*
I gotta nice place. *Kaspoit!* Don't vant nobody poking around.

Well. *Kaspoit!* Between the remotitude. The cameras. The fence. And good ole Fritzie there. I'd say you pretty much got it covered.

Ja I vish it vere true. Da goddamn Ruckmumps ver around here yesterday.

Yeah?

Say dey gotta varrant. Impossibla. Djust bullshitting dats all. I got no varrant. Dey never catch me. Dey never know vhat I am doing. Dey say dey know about my gun biznez. Dey know nuttink. Dey talking tru dere asses ja.

MonsterFace furrowDark. The cops were here yesterday?

One lady constable dats all dey send. Schtoopit! I tol her I cut her clean in half she comes any closer.

She was right up in here?

I stop her right on da road. She get novhere near.

Jeeze Rude. I'd hate to think you'd turned into a heatbag.

Donchu vorry. If you are all fired up unt ready to go you can get your guns unt finish your beer unt bugger off. Dozzen madder to me.

That would likely be the best idea for now. *FurrowFace look-About.* I imagine Roberto got in touch?

Ja Roberto. You guys need zum zimple stuff ja.

Simple yeah. *HulkSniff.* But they wouldn't let us on the plane with it.

TriCorner horkLaugh.

Kommen sie hier.

TrioTrudge rearMarch.

AutoPart dissembleLitter.

ArmourHeavy weldBound cubeVan.

LightField pieceCannon.

ToolGallery machineArt:
drillPress
latheTurn
punchHole
spotWeld

compressAir
acetylTorch cutWand.
VastLitter oddEnd nutBolt drillBit storeMass.
MetalDrawer yankRough. I set dese out for you guys.
HeftHold stepCarry thudPlace jeepHood.

Man. *HulkAwe.* Nice stuff.

Ja I got all da best. Unt vhat is not za best I make za best.

HulkNod. I see you carry Auto Ordinance.

Ja za 1911A series. All models. I vork on dem as you see.
Clean as can be. No numbers. Nuttink less dan fortyfive calibre.

HandGrip gunBrandish rackSlide. Hear dat? Not much
sound ja. I lubricate za joints and damp zee action for added
stealth. Now za silencer. *TwistBarrel.* You try zilencing a
bruiser like dis gun ja. Near impossibla. Bud I do it.

RangeLook. See dat oilcan on za bench? *SnapLevel aimSight.*
SputSlight.

OverLoud canFling.

Not bad Rude. *HulkHand gunHeft.* We'll need one each of
course.

Ja.

And we like to work with a lighter piece for backup and
custom jobs. Whattya got?

Boot guns eh? Zee here. *HeftLift.* Best is za Beretta. Vhat
you vant? Twentytwo? Twentyfive? Tirdytwo?

Twentyfive.

Here you go den. *PistolHeft.* Goot for holstering. Secreting.
Goot backup shooter dis.

Hey Rude. You got enhanced ammo for all this stuff?

Ja I got dat. *DrawerPull.* Dere. Boxes each. Dat stuff vill pen-
etrate any armour now. Da kevlar and all da rest. Can't guaran-
tee next year but right now ja. Dey vorkink on zumpting called
dragonskin now. I hear anyvay. Close veave texdile viss
zeramic plating. Stop everytink apparently. I donno. Za biznez
keeps me jumpink.

BlareHorn.

Whatthefuckissat?
BlareHorn. BlareHorn.
FaceDark. Scheise!
BlareHorn. BlareHorn. BlareHorn.
StepSwift backOffice. Zomeone at za gate.
BlareHorn.
BlareHorn.
FistHit redKnob.
BlareStop.
TrioHulk cramOffice.
SecuriConsole.
Black&White lectroImage.
HatHeavy policeHead fishEye wideView.
Scheise! Scheise! Scheise!
BackGround shadowMoves.
Verdammen sie polizei!
Shitflames!
FaceFurrow. You understand Rudy we can't be found in.
DeadTone killVoice. This has to get dealt with.

Ja ja ja. *KeyPunch dataJab.* I lock down za gate and shut za systems. No lights no nuttink. Dey tink I am gone ja.

It better fucken work.
ScreenImage toolWield.
Scheise!
LockPost zapShot.
BlankBlack teleFeed.

PanicShuffle. Scheise scheise scheise. *ShopStride.* Very vell zen. You guyz ged out an hide in za trees. I handle zese foolish berzons. *CrateOpen.*

Holy fuck!
MachineArmy colossoGun.
Nussink holy aboud dis detspitter mein friends. *TrainCannon.*
Whattzat a fucken thirty cal?

Dey won't gedda chance to see vhat it is. *ColdEye wideStand armFlex.* Now grab dose guns unt ged out dere unt obzerve.

HulkGunning. He effen means it man.
I'd say so.
I'll meet dem here. *EngineBlock downDuck.*
MonsterFlee.
Guess we're gonna gun it out.
No other way.
DuoHulk speedLoad.
BushCrawl.
CalmPause.
BirdSong.
BreezeRustle treeHiss.
SylvanStill.
BreezeRustle.
MotorNoise faintLight.
MotorNoise.
FordUte copConvoy.
PauseWait.
EngineOff. EngineOff.
DoorSwing.
DoorSwing.
DoorSwing.
DoorSwing.
ArmourUniform scatterGun subMachine pistolPack.
Mister Meuller!
SoundPause.
BirdTweet.
TreeWind.
Mister Meuller!
BirdTweet.
TwoRank weaponBristle slowWalk.
Rudolph Wilhelm Meuller! We have a warrant for your arrest.
NoSound slowPace.
HangarLoose dogGallop.
ShotGun fireSmoke.
Yelp! *TurnTail dogLimp.*

Mister Meuller please step out of the hangar.
PauseWait.
CopHuddle whisperTalk.
TreeBreeze.
BirdTweet.
Mister Meuller for the last time. *DuoCop leadCop breakOff slowWalk.* Show yourself. *HangarClose.* Stand up and walk out. Keep your hands to your sides.
RoarBurst.
HideHulks earCover.
MurderDin.
LeadRank redMist flyLimb.
EndBurst.
RearRank scrambleSide.
HulkRise twoHand standCombat.
FortyfiveFire.
DownUniforms.
GrimHulk victimSide downLook. HeadFire.
MonsterAim.
No man. Hold up a sec.
Wha? *DownAim.* He's still breathin.
Hold up a sec.
You know the rules man.
Yeah yeah.
No witnesses.
Yeah yeah but.
But what?
We got time. Things are moving too fast. Let's work this out.
KillerDuo standClose.
Okay. *SquatFlame handPull officerGlock.*
VictimMoan.
What's to work out?
How we're gonna play this.
You think we can tweak it?
NodMonster. Let us review. *HeadPoint.* Rudy does for those

two over there with his effen doomsday gun. Results are fucken plain to see.

I'll fucken tell the world.

Then has a casual firefight with the two we have lying here. Yeah.

He runs out of ammo for the cannon and switches to these. *Pistol Heft*. Fortyfive cal semi automatic Auto Ordinance 1911A series rods. The kind he likes to deal in.

And that the cops likely know he's got.

Right you are.

So he firefights it out with these guys.

One in each hand. *Hulk Stand*. He bang bang bangs away. *Pistol Aim. Chest Fire.*

Still Uniform.

Now with this. *Police Gun heft Wave*. Good old Glock nine millimetre. Before the cop kicks on account of the two that got through his vest armour he whacks Rudy. Right?

I see it. *Furrow Face mental Work*. It's not gonna be airtight.

Oh hell no. But it'll buy us at least as much time as we need.

Not bad Flame my boy. Reminds me why I can stand to hang around you.

One of us have to have some brains.

Fuck you.

And back again. So aside from all this fun conversation we'll have to get going.

It'll take some scrounging.

You're not kidding. First. These fortyfives to Rudy. Second. This Glock back in the cop's hand. *Hulk Swivel round Look*. Footprints might be a hitch but there's a zillion of em anyway. The only obvious factor is tiretracks. We'll have to drive back out. Careful not to overroll the cop vehicle tracks if we possibly can. Then we walk back in and get treebranches or something.

Don't forget the cameras. Think he has video?

Here he comes. Let's ask him.

Hey Rude. You okay?

Dey shod my fuggen dock.

Yeah. That was cold.

He whimperink and limpink around like a zirgus glown.

You better not send em the vet bill.

WipeHand shakeWrist earCup. Can't ear you.

No?

Ja. *ThroatHack.* Dat thirty is za vorst ting in za vorld to fire visout a tripod unt a pair of earmuffs. And za cordite gas nearly choke you.

Well you did a fine job on those first two.

I can barely ear you. Za noise.

I SAY YOU DID A FINE JOB ON THOSE FIRST TWO RUDY.

Vhat did you do mit za ones who ran?

See for yourself.

Ja.

TrioSpectate.

Hey by the way Rude. You got video in any of those cameras?

Video? Vhat za hell would I vant dat for? I got zatellite free. I got a touzand channels I can't vatch it all.

Hah. Gotcha.

So you see. *HulkFinger corpsePoint.* Rudy. We got these guys.

Ja gud.

Your vest punching ammo really did the job.

Ja. As I said. Dis year maybe not next year.

Well Rude that's the thing. This year's all we care about.

You young guys.

Yeah that's right. Us young guys. Never thinking about the future.

Vell you bedder schtart.

Ha ha. Actually you don't know how right you are.

Vhat?

So Rudy. *NodPoint.* Stand about there wouldya?

Dere? Vhy should I stand dere? I can see gud from here.

Well I guess that's okay. *GunArm GlockRaise quickFire.*
BrainShot downBody.
And good fucken riddance!
The nerve of this goof exposing us to this kinda heat.
Yer effen eh. *SneerMonster.* It fucken boggles.
I'm gonna have a word with Roberto.
Effen eh.
Complete bullshit.

NIGHT; FIRESIDE: BOOZECAN

SmokeFire monsterCircle swillScene.
HulkCan fireFling.
Kaspoit!
SidleMonster HulkSide.
Hey Gort.
Scroat.
You got enougha those to spare?
Here. *CanToss.* Enjoy.
Thanks. *Kaspoit!* So. *SwillGulp.* You gonna do her?
Maybe. Somethin. But either way. She'll fucken remember.
Effen eh. Broads eh?
Fucken broads.
So what is it she supposedly did exactly?
Smashed the windshield on my Vette for fuck sakes!
You see her do it?
Didn't have to. Nobody else around here is crazy enough.
That's for sure.
Claimed I killed her fucken dog.
Hah!
Stuff gettin outta control around this shithouse.
No effen question about it.
Gotta put in a little discipline.
Truth be told.
Fucken outrage.
You let this stuff go. *SwillGulp.* Shitstorm.
Not if I got a fucken hand in it.
Absofuckenlutely.
ShadowMonster shiftStand hulkSide. Hey Gort.
Hey Geekster.

You sposed to be runnin this shithouse?

Uh huh. I think you know that already.

Just so's ya know. I heard Roberto's gonna shake things up.

You did huh.

Place is fallin apart eh.

I'm sprised you'd notice.

Fuck you.

Fuck you too.

Hey you fucken guys. *GrabCans.* Chug these fucken things and let's get down to fucken work okay.

SnortSniff. Go the fuck ahead.

Here.

Here.

Kaspoit! Kaspoit! Kaspoit!

Maybe not solve anything. *HulkChug.* But I never turn down a fucken beer.

Hey Geek. Maybe instead of complaining all the time you might like to help with the problem.

Why would I wanna do that?

The fucken fun factor. *HorkLaugh.*

What the fuck you guys talkin about?

Come the fuck on. *PowerChug. CanToss.* We got work to do and you just might be the kinda expert we need.

TrioMarch crossMud.

BrownBarn.

ArmFling doorWide.

LowBurn rafterBeam hangBulb.

DogStink.

MuffleMoan.

DuctTape limbBound backProne shiverNude.

Holy shit. You fuckers don't fool around do ya?

This ugly fucken fat skank smashed my windshield. She's not leavin here alive.

Effen eh.

Where the fuck is Friendly? *ShadowSearch.*

I told the ignorant fuck to be here.

What's he got to do with it?

This my good man is his fucken sister. Didn't you know that?

Friendly has a sister? Fuck me what a fucked up life she musta had.

The question is what kinda fucked up life is she gonna have? If any.

So why we waitin for Friendly? I never met a fucken boringer guy.

For this to have any meaning it has to be witnessed. Preferably a family member.

Geekster my man. *MachetePull*. Take this. And do something disciplinary with it.

Whoa you fucks are into somethin radical here.

Thought you'd think so. Gimme a beer Scroaty.

Kaspoit! My last one guys. *SwillGulp grinWatch*.

Fuck me. *PhoneSearch pocketWhip*. Forgot to bring fucken beer. Gotta make this occasion perfect. *StabDial*. Hey Friendly? Wheredafuckareya? Yeah. Yeah. Your sister's here. In the barn. We toldja. Get the fuck over here. Right fucken now. That's right. Okay. Wait a minute don't hang up. Don't fucken hang up! Okay now we want sumpm. Yeah. Two six-packs. Yeah. Two. Two times six equals twelve got it? Make em cold. We don't want em warm. Get over here. Right now. Yeah. *PhoneFold*.

Fuck. How does a bitch get so fat?

She is a porker isn't she.

Put a guy off bacon.

Fuck my ol lady gets that fat I'm fucken kickin er out.

Jeeze can you imagine some guys fuck things like this?

Hell some guys like em like this.

Some guys just got no fucken self-respect.

I knew a guy once he'd leapfrog over some hot slim chick and go for hogsbreath here. I'm not fucken kiddin.

I can't fucken imagine.

Hey stranger fucken shit under the sun buddy.

Nevermind the flab I can't stand the smell.

Yeah what is that? I thought it was the animals.

They don't keep animals in here anymore. Just dogs.

It's worse than dogs.

Wet filthy rolled in shit dog.

I donno. There's a rot smell too. I wonder where it's comin from.

Dammit my scent smellin nose. This whole fucken compound is fulla rot. I can't pick out any peticular part.

Well as far as yer nose is concerned don't pick any peticular part. It's fucken disgustin.

Ha ha.

RattleShed. What the fuck is goin on?

Bout time Friendly. Why the fuck weren't you here?

Because Gort. I didn't wanna be here.

Gimme onea those sixpacks.

BeerToss. Whattya got Rosa all trussed up for?

Rosa's gonna get her snatch reamed for smashing the fucken windshield on my fucken Vette.

She didn't mean it. She was upset about Sidewinder.

Kaspoit! She fucken gave me nothin but lip this afternoon.

Didn't you ever lose somethin you loved?

Aw jeeze I'm gonna start cryin here if I don't get this beer down and Geeksterman there doesn't do somethin with that machete in his hand.

Come on you guys let go my sister.

Shut the eff up you fucken lameass. Who the fuck you think calls the shots around here?

I don't care.

Same people who pay the bills.

I don't give a darn who pays what. You got no right to hurt my sister. *LashLunge flingSix.* Now let her go!

Settle the fuck down. *TeamRestraint.* And be careful with that beer.

You fucken guys!
I'll get this over quick. *Squat Pose.*
Crotch Nexus.
Machete Touch.
Aw fuck! *Back Stumble.*
Femme Spasm splash Brown.
The fucken broad shit at me!
Hork Laugh. She hit you?
No she fucken shit at me.
I say again did she hit you? With the shit.
Fuck nearly.
Well then.
The fucken smell.
Let's get the fuck outta here.
I can't fucken stand it.
Laugh Monsters.
Stagger Run.
Before I fucken puke.
It's gonna be close.
Open the fucken door.
Jog Monster. Phew. Fucken fresh air.
I thought I'd fucken lose my good steak dinner.
Blade Swing. Well some fucken executioners we turned out
to be.
Throw that fucken jackknife away.
Fire Ward arm Fling machete Toss.
Spark Fly.
You know what you should do with that smelly cunt.
What should I do with that smelly cunt?
Make her go with Friendly on his hooker runs.
What's the fucken logica that?
The girls get spooked by the fucken freak's appearance. Not
to mention the smell.
They both got that problem.
Yeah but she at least can get them into the car easier.

Bitches trust bitches in that situation more than they trust a hairy stinkin bizarro in a thrapped out station wagon.

Hmm. *FurrowBrow.* You might have somethin there.

Think about it.

I am.

And hand me a beer.

Here's two.

Whoa what's the occasion?

Yer fucken good idea. Got any more of em there's more beer in it for ya.

Don't mention it. *Kaspoit!*

Gimme one too whydontcha? *HulkReach.*

Here ya go Scroat.

Kaspoit! SwillGuzzle.

SwillGuzzle. GulpSigh.

GlanceAround.

Who're those guys?

Which guys?

Over there. The two by the gangfuck. The ones with the shiny collarpin thingamajigs.

Doze guys? *TalkDrink gazeMonster.* I donno.

Those guys? *CanHand slantPoint.* Those guys are the guys Roberto brought in.

Oh yeah?

From back east.

Oh yeah. He mentioned em yesterday.

Killers.

How you know Scroat?

I just do.

Pistol packers?

Stone fucken killers.

And Roberto brought em in?

Yup.

For what?

Oh. *SideGlance.* That little thing.

What little thing? *SideLook*. Oh yeah.

You know.

Yeah I know. A problem.

A little problem. Or somethin. Roberto thinks it should get the serious treatment.

Yeah yeah. The border pinch.

Yeah that and some other stuff. Roberto's lookin to get it all done with.

With those guys? What's he got in mind?

I'm not sposed ta say.

Effen fine with me.

Wish I didn't know either. I donno why he's gettin so excited.

Yeah. Like. There's other stuff goin on.

That's for damn sure. Shit happenin all over the place.

I got nothin but trouble.

Naw rilly?

All over the fucken place.

The rental outfit?

Naw that's goin good.

The grow?

That's fine too. But.

What then?

Well the ole lady situation.

Oh fuck. Marital shit isn't my department.

Wish it wasn't mine neither.

Just do with it the best you can. My advice.

I'm tryin.

I mean. We all got enough stuff goin on without getting all jammed up with each other's bitch situation.

I'll say.

Fucken business is already a couplea handfuls too many.

Yeah I guess.

That reminds me. Did Friendly get those school wrecks for ya?

The Winnipeg Flyers?

Whatever the fuck those yellow busses are called.

He got me some Flyers. Yer thinkin about Blue Birds. Whatever.

I got somea those too. The school board auction. Think I'm gonna convert ta freight containers though. Busses are getting to be a real hassle. Had to outbid some greasy Guatemalan transportation dudes.

What the fucker ya talkin about?

HulkSmirk. You don't know this stuff because you never got yer hands green farmin pot. *Kaspoit! SwillGulp.* You have to get these tanked out old school busses before they go to some shithouse banana country. *BurpMonster.*

Yer shittin me.

I seen em do it man. Guy showed me a pitjer of how they fuck with em. Redo the suspension. Supercharge the motor. And the decorations. Fuck man they dress em up like Christmas trees. Firstclass superhighway fucken public transportation.

Go ta fucken hell.

I'm not kiddin.

They got a public bus line?

Oh that's the real wacky part. Get this. It's totally wide open. No law. No government. No cops. No nothin. They drive up and down the fucken highway and country roads and cow trails and footpaths and anywhere they can think of to go and pick up people and take em somewhere. Anywhere. No timetables. No routes. They just drive. One guy at the wheel. Another guy hawking the passengers up off the road and onto the bus. He also loads shit up on the roof. All kindsa stuff apparently. Includin animals. Whatever the fucken hell. And collects the fares.

Until they get loaded and head to town I guess.

According to this cat they never do get loaded. I mean there's no maximum capacity. If there's somebody walkin along and they get flagged down the policy is to pick em up regardless. You see these pictures of people hanging off the sides. Arms hooked in the windows. Holding on up top. Seventy passenger bus can have like two hundred people on it.

No fucken way.

Fucken way man. That's why when you hear about bus crashes in these poorhouse toiletbowls there's always a huge deathcount. Like they never have an accident where like one person gets killed and a couple of people are hurt or something like that. They always have these humungous disasters where some teenage drunken hyped-on-meth speed maniac races the fucken thing over a cliff and kills like sixty or a hundred people in one foul swoop so to fucken speak.

Fucken insanity.

Yeah fuck. *UrpSlurp*. Maybe we're doin em a favour.

How so?

By usin these fucken deathtraps for buried greenhouses.

Hah. Maybe. Who gives a fuck.

I sure as fucken don't.

Atta boy. You got an important function there.

Effen eh.

You're what they call yer economic engine.

Right on mofo.

Hey by the way. Where you livin these days?

Still at the site.

What! Didn't Roberto tell you to get the fuck outta there?

Yeah but I got no place else to go. Sheila threw me out of the condo.

What the fucker ya talkin about?

My ol lady. She—

I know who the fuck your ol lady is and what the fuck she did with ya I'm just askin what the fuck you think you're doin living overtop a fucken grow op?

I'm outta there next week.

Effen eh you are. Fucken stupid you ask me.

That's what Roberto said.

You're lucky he doesn't do more than just say.

I hear ya bro.

You better. This is serious shit here.

Gotcha.

Sweet effen heyzoose. You gotta get outta there.

I fucken know.

Fucken heatscore.

Don't I know it.

And whatter ya lettin yer ol lady kick ya outta yer own effen house for anyway?

She was pissed at me for the border thing. Her mother don't like jailbirds.

Fuck her and fuck her mother.

You wouldn't want to man.

HulkLaugh. Kaspoit!

GroupUrine fireHiss.

HulkDrone.

DrinkChat. Kaspoit!

HulkSidle duoMonster. Which onea you guys is Gort?

Whoodda fucker you?

Guests. From back east.

Oh yeah. Onea you guys's name is Fire?

Flame. I'm Chico.

Well howdy.

You're Gort?

Yup.

HorkLaugh. Klaatu barada nikto. *HulkSnort.*

Fucken funny bud. Guess I never heard that one eh?

How'd you get such a classic?

My fucken drunken retard buddies in first grade couldn't pronounce Gord. Or spell it. Or somethin. I doen remember.

HulkFrown. What the fuck language you guys talkin?

C'mon Scroat. You don't watch movies? You never seen *The Day the Earth Stood Still*?

Uh maybe. Who was in it?

Nevermind.

Hey. Your name Scroaty?
Yeah.
We got business. *GrimKiller upStep.* Roberto sent us.
Yeah. Okay. Can we get at this tomorrow?
Why not now?
Friendly's van just pulled in. Hookers.
Hookers?
Maybe even enough to go around. Yeah.
Sufferin slamfuck boyos. Whores! Wherdafuck do we get em?
I guess I'm the fucken hospitality committee. *CanWave.*
Roberto told me to take carea you guys.
Fucken great. *KillerLeer.* So howzit with them hookers?
LeadMonster. Come the fuck on fellers.

MORNING; WEEDFARM: WHACKMEN

WeedFarm ramShack.
CouchHulk.
SpeedChannel surfShift.
AmericaFunny policeChase. ClickShift.
Playboy gynoFest. ClickShift.
GorePlastic fatSurgery. ClickShift.
BlackWhite movieNoir. ClickShift.
SuperCycle chopperBuild.
ClickShift clickShift.
CrazyChef ironCook.
ClickShift. CanGrab.
Kaspoit!
TiltGulp. ClickShift. TiltGulp.
MotoSound.
RemoteKill canDrop. LeapLook windowCrack.
SquintView.
SedanPark.
FemmeStand. BriefCase.
HouseWard mudStep.
Aw fuck lady why dontcha turn around and go back right
now huh? *HulkSpy.* Yer gonna ruin yer shoes.
DoorKnock.
SlowOpen doorSwing.
Mr. Skutowski?
Uh huh.
I'm Janis McReedy from court services?
Uh huh.
Here to do your pre-sentence report?
Okay.

I spoke to you on the phone?

Yup.

Ummm. *RoomGaze*. This is going to take some time. Can we sit down?

Oh. Sure. *HulkStep*. I kinda hoped we could postpone this thing.

You said so on the phone. *DownGlance grimeCarpet*. As I explained. The sentencing has to take place next week? We're already rilly late?

Yeah yeah. But I'm movin soon.

To another house or another district?

Another house.

Well then that has little bearing on what we're doing here today Mr. Skutowski. Now then. The kitchen table?

Yeah yeah. *HulkLead*.

My my. It looks like you never throw anything away.

Huh?

Your house is rilly cluttered if you don't mind me saying.

Oh yeah. I gotta clean up some day.

Some day soon I would imagine.

Huh?

If you're moving.

Oh yeah. Yeah. *ArmSweep tableKitchen clearWipe*. Here good enough?

Fine. Ooh classic diner style linoleum. And this surface looks like authentic fifties retro arborite. You don't see that very much anymore. These old farmhouses are so much fun.

Yeah.

Okay. I'll just get my stuff out here? Have you ever spoken to a court services person before?

Nope.

You were a probationer once weren't you?

Yeah.

Well that counts. You'd have had to have spoken to some-one? As well as your probation officer.

That was back in Ontario.

When you were a juvie. *FilePage*. In Bewdley. That's a town north of Toronto. Right?

Yeah. I was a juvie in Bewdley.

Oh that's good. You can joke about it. Humour is good.

If you say so.

And what got you to be a juvie in Bewdley was mainly property and drugs?

Yup.

Were you a little hellion?

What's that?

A bad little boy.

Yeah sure. Me an every other self-respecting kid.

Would you say you existed in a criminal milieu?

What the fuck is that?

Environment. *TalkScribble*. Family atmosphere. *ScribbleTalk*. Peer group dynamics.

I donno what the fuck you're talkin about.

I'll explain in greater detail? But first. *EyeHold*. Let's get our tombstone data straight?

What's that?

Name birthdate birthplace parental info et cetera. Essentially I just have to verify what's in the file? You wouldn't believe how inaccurate arrest info can be. *FileFlip*. Your name is Feodor Lancelot Skutowski. s-k-u-t-o-w-s-k-i.

Umm yeah.

Your parents were of Eastern European background?

Croatia.

That sounds appropriately ethnic. But your middle name?

Mom was a King Arthur fan.

Oh that's cool. *ScribbleNod*.

People just call me Scroaty.

EyeWide. They call you what?

Scroaty.

Scroaty?

Yup.

Well. I won't be doing that.

Suit yerself.

How about I call you by your first name?

Whatever.

May I refer to you as Feodor?

Sure.

Great. You can call me Jan. *FileRead.* And your birthdate is October 16. Thirty. *BrowFurrow.* Eight years ago?

Yeah. I guess.

Okay. And I can see that you are a white male of husky physique. Hazel eyes. What colour would your hair be if you had any?

Brown.

What would you say you weigh? About a hundred?

Fuck I donno.

A hundred kilos I would estimate.

Whatever that is.

Around two twenty. Two twenty-five in pounds.

I guess so.

And about what height? One ninety?

Huh?

Centimetres.

I donno.

Five feet eight?

Five nine.

Fine. *CellPhone pocketPull.* I have to figure out exactly how many metres that is. If I can only remember how to activate the calculator function on this thing. *FingerKey padJab.* Okay. I think I got it. One point seven five three. Does that sound right to you?

Fucked if I know.

Feodor can I make just a tiny request?

Go ahead.

If you don't mind could you keep the profanity to a minimum during our interview? I realize you're not used to being told how to speak but I rilly must insist you try to keep a civil mouth on you? *Scribble Write*. Okay?

Whatever.

Sorry to lay it out to you like that. But it's important to maintain a professional atmosphere? Sometimes?

It's okay.

Thank you. Now then. As you know. At your appearance before Justice Bender last month you pleaded guilty to one count of possession for the purpose of trafficking and one count of attempt to import a narcotic. Is that right?

You know it.

Feodor I must get you to answer my questions directly. It's an important part of the disclosure process? Do you understand?

Yeah sure I'm not stupid. I did it eh.

Fine. Now the judge ordered this pre-sentence report because aside from the juvie stuff which took place more than twenty years ago now you've lived crime free? In these circumstances that's kind of unusual? I mean as a rule a person caught with more cocaine than any mortal person could use in a decade usually has more of a criminal background?

It wasn't mine.

You pleaded guilty. If the stuff wasn't yours you should have pleaded not guilty.

It's like you said. I'm a first offender. I just wanted to get the eff out of there.

I don't think it's going to be quite that simple. A kilo is a lot. And the fact it was found in your car as you tried to take it across the border complicates things considerably. Too bad you didn't get to explain that in court.

Yeah. Too bad.

Usually this kind of smuggling gets done in more sophisticated ways.

Oh yeah?

I sense you know that already.

Sense away lady.

Forgive me for supposing that that was the real reason you copped a plea. You didn't want to explain.

Think what you wanna think.

Okay. Well. We're not here to get to the bottom of that mystery but if you should feel the urge to just blurt something out while we're talking about other things I promise I won't interrupt you.

That's okay.

So I guess we should get started?

Aren't we already?

How do you make your living?

I got a car alarm company.

You install car alarms?

Yup.

Do you have a shop somewhere?

Langley city.

What's the address?

Sixteenth street and something.

What's the number?

Can't remember. I just go there.

Are you adept at mechanics?

I dunno. I guess.

Do you do this work personally?

I got some guys.

Is the shop open right now?

I got a manager.

How often do you go to the business?

Twice a week or so.

Oh? Your manager is a trustworthy fellow I take it.

He better be.

Any other source of income?

Nope.

It says here. *EyeDown scanFile.* You have partial title in a condo development in Abbotsford.

Yeah. So?

That would be a source of income wouldn't it?

Sometimes. I don't rilly handle it.

So you have a management company administer the property?

Management company? I guess. My partners see to it.

Well. That's pretty convenient. What about the tire shop?

What tire shop?

The one out in Mission. It says here you've owned the place for five years.

Oh that thing. Yeah. I sold it.

There's no record of a transfer of title.

I'm handing it off to a guy who works for me.

Would that be the same person who manages Deadman Specialty Choppers?

Uh.

High-end motorcycle manufacturing and modification. Five thousand square metre plant with sales North America wide.

Uh.

Last year the company grossed eleven million dollars.

Uh.

Are you saying yes with that grunt or are you just not answering?

How much did you say the gross was?

Eleven million.

No kiddin?

Feodor let's stop kidding ourselves. You've done well in the drug business haven't you?

What are you implyin?

What do you think?

Where'd ya get all that stuff?

Research.

You guys must work pretty hard.

Feodor I'll come clean if you come clean. Okay?

Whaddya mean?

I'll tell you something important if you tell me something important.

I donno.

Well whatever. Most of this info. *LiftFile deadDrop*. Came from police informant sources. Tons of them. Over years. Mostly from people who are now dead.

No kiddin.

You know I'm not.

I don't hardly know nothin.

Well surely you don't think we're all idiots?

Toldya. I wouldn't know.

Do you think a person who we know barely leaves his house. Has a Grade Nine education. Can barely remember his own business address. Whose friends nickname him after a saggy part of the male anatomy. Never dresses in anything other than a bowling shirt or a leather jacket. And gets caught coming through the border with a blow-filled pillowcase could logically be accepted as a millionaire business tycoon?

I shoulda got my lawyer here.

You don't need your lawyer here. None of this is provable. The police won't let us use it. And I didn't Charter you. Everything we discuss is inadmissible except as it pertains to sentencing. And, as you say, you're essentially a first-timer. But I will make a point of noting you are a man of means. No matter how you got it. I suppose you should be proud.

You're a fucken weird broad.

And impervious to flattery Feodor and please remember to watch your mouth. Now because you pleaded guilty the court knows little about the background of your offence. Do you wish to try to mitigate the thus inevitably negative perception of the court by explaining how it was you were traveling with such a loaded piece of bedding?

I'm not sayin nothin.

As I expected. So we leave the mitigation section empty.

Are there any other circumstances that you would wish the court to consider?

Huh?

Were you beaten as a child?

Well sure. But.

I'll need details.

Naw forget about it.

You're certain about that?

Yeah.

What about relationships. Are you married?

I got an ol lady.

Is she here?

Naw she lives in a condo in Chilliwack. I'm movin there.

Is that the place on 10th Street listed here on the arrest sheet as your home address?

Yeah.

Well why are you living here now?

I'm not. I'm just stayin here temporary.

That's not what I was told on the phone. Your "old lady," as you put it, told me you were here and she didn't care if she ever saw you again dead or alive.

Fucken loopy bitch. She's just pissed off.

May I ask why?

Oh lotsa stuff.

My impression is that she isn't letting you back into the relationship. Or the condo.

She'll come around.

Well for the purposes of this report you understand I must state things as I find them. If there are variations in the interim you can report them to the court at the time of your appearance.

Yeah yeah.

So. Any other relationships? Family? Friends?

Naw.

No family?

Naw.

No friends?

Naw.

Oh come on now. Feodor. You must have somebody you hang out with.

BlearEye. I said no and I mean no.

Okay then. You don't have to get heavy about it. *FileScribble.* Okay if that's all there is to talk about we'll just get on with the residence inspection and then we'll be done.

Inspection?

As I explained to you over the phone Feodor. I need to see what conditions you are living under with specific attention to signs you might be involved in the drug trade.

Yeah?

So you know I need to walk around your place here and write out a physical description for the court.

I'm not gonna be livin here by the time I get to court.

You mentioned that several times. And I explained to you several times that that is immaterial to the pre-sentence procedure. It's clear you've been occupying this place for some time. Municipal records indicate your parents purchased it in nineteen seventy-seven and left it to you on their passing. And you don't indicate any other addresses in the intervening years. So it's rilly your home base. Your true roots. No matter where you might temporarily or otherwise relocate.

I'm leavin this place tomorrow an I'm never comin back.

I find it strange that you say that. Is there some kind of painful memory or association here?

Naw naw. I just doen wanna live here no more.

Oh. Okay. I hope things work out for you. Sometimes a geographical change is as good as a cure. Leave the past behind. Make a new start. But I still have to take a walk around.

I'm advisin ya not to.

If you don't comply a warrant will be issued and you'll have the place covered with RCMP by mid-afternoon.

Oh fuck.

Language.

Have it your way.

It's rilly for the better. I don't mind telling you. You wouldn't believe how eager they are to do just that. Crawl all over the place. The police.

You don't say.

I do say. In fact they wanted me to tell you that specifically.

No shit.

Don't sit there and tell me you're surprised.

Fuck I doen know nothin bout the cops. Never talk to em.

Well they seem to know you.

Don't know what the fuck's goin on.

Well whatever. *FileFold*. Time to get on with it. *StandRise caseGrab*. Show me your big spread here.

There's nothin to see.

Oh I disagree. You've got how many acres? Twenty-five?

Twenty-seven if you count the marsh. Nobody goes there.

Well for a place that used to be far from the city and now is only just a three minute drive off the freeway you must have seen many changes.

Huh?

Nevermind.

DuoTrudge.

CrossDrive sludgePuddle mudSpan.

Do you always have such deep muck? I'm glad I wore my hikers.

Tol ya not to come.

All in a day's work Feodor. *FarPoint*. Is all that yours?

Yeah up to the treeline. And that hill beyond over there. See the cellphone tower?

Uh huh.

Well just past that.

Impressive.

Okay you seen it all now so now you go eh.

I have to inspect your outbuildings.

You doen wanna do that.

Mr. Skutowski do we have to go through all this again?

Aw jeesh.

There's rilly no other way.

Aw fer fucksakes. Come on then. Knock yerself out.

You certainly have a lot of earth moving equipment over there.

I do a little contracting.

Why didn't you say so? *StopStride. ScribbleNote.* I have to see that building there.

Which one?

Well all of them. But especially that one with the big vent thingies on top.

Why don't you look in all of em but that one?

I won't dignify that with an answer.

HulkHand metalKnob.

Wait a sec. *NoseWrinkle airSniff.* What's that smell?

What? You mean skunks?

Skunk is one smell. This is another.

I don't smell nothin.

Cannabis. It is isn't it?

Yer dreamin.

There it is again. *SmellBreath.* It comes in waves.

It's those guys livin over there. *FarPoint.*

Over where?

That outfit over there. They smoke from mornin til night.

You mean that house with the van parked outside?

Yeah.

They're at least half a kilometre away.

Stuff carries.

Hmm. *NoseFlex.* I don't know about that. This smells.
NoseFlex. There it is again. This smells like fresh. Not smoke.
NoseFlex. Effluvium. As they call it.

Yer fucken crazy lady.

Now Feodor I can't help thinking you're doing something

which involves cannabis here because there is a distinctive smell. Can you explain that to me?

I'm tellin ya I don't have nothin to do with the stuff no more. *FumbleKey lockOpen doorSwing.*

It's even stronger in here. *StepTalk.* Can you turn on a light?

I got no power in here.

Are you sure? What are those photography lamps doing in the corner?

Not connected.

This place rilly stinks.

Maybe it's sweetgrass you're smellin. I smudged the place. It's all got to do with native spirituality.

What?

Like the Indians do. Ya set fire to these dry weeds and scare away all the evil spirits. Smells zackly like weed.

Forgive me for chuckling. I don't recall any reference in the file material about you being aboriginal. And frankly Feodor. You don't look anything like a First Nations person.

I learned about it in juvie.

TalkStep. What's this plastic sheet doing on the floor? *HeadTurn.*

I guess I. *WordChoke.*

ShadowMonster.

ThinBarrel skullTrain.

SputSpeak.

AmmoOccipital cerebrumPunch.

EyeBug lifeHalt.

KneeLoose eyeRoll.

DownFemme.

This was what? *OutStep KillHulk.*

TwentyfiveSmoke.

A cop?

Naw. Some fucken court reporter type.

Well. *HulkOver standBy.* Damn. She ain't bad lookin. We shoulda fucked her.

Go right ahead.

Naw I'm not into necro.

Stupid bitch. *SweepArm*. We'da had all this fucken shit moved outta here by next week. But she wouldn't fucken listen.

Isn't that the fuckenest? *KillerChuckle*. A bitch who won't listen. More dead bitches in the world dead because they wouldn't listen than any other fucken reason. No?

Fucken right.

Effen eh.

Fucken sad but true man.

Okay now. *KillGrave*. In any case. You see Scroaty how we arranged it so she'd be spread across this sheet of poly?

Yeah.

We're here to help you out bud. So we're gonna show you just exactly what to do. First. Check her for a cell phone and or Blackberry and or any other electronic shit she might have and that might trace to her. Then this briefcase here. Empty it and smash it and burn it and bag it and throw it in the trunk of her car. Then use this here hatchet and take her head off and her hands off and put em in this here garbage bag.

Huh?

Get choppin.

I don't do that kinda shit.

Hey look. Me an Flame are busy too. We gotta go over her car. Make sure there's nothing traceable. We gotta go get the fiveton. Drive the bitch's car up into it. Gotta wipe out all the tracks. Get it down the road to the crusher without being seen. Et cetera cetera. This is teamwork. No time to fucken waste here.

Can't we just throw her in a fucken hole?

Sure we could. And a fine long rest it would be for the three of us. Sittin in some federal scungejoint for the next ten years or so until we make parole.

Shit.

A stiff's the easiest thing to find these days. Gas detectors.

Dogs. Radar. Airborne heat sensitive digital photography. And the forensic cops got all the science on their side. A fucken body like this is as good as a confession.

Yeah maybe.

No maybe about it.

But choppin her head off. I don't fucken know.

Don't you watch TV Scroaty?

Not much.

Well if you did you'd appreciate what Flame and me are doing for ya here. In the interest of plausible deniability you know. Ever hearda that?

Naw.

Well it's important to have if you're gonna go whacking cops and court people et cetera like you got here. I mean look at all the care we've taken. First of all you'll notice we used small calibre. Little or no spatter. Only thing shot is her brain and not your far wall over there. Nice and neat. She flumps down on this easy to fold up poly sheet here. This also makes for a convenient work surface. Now under our direction you get rid of her identifying features and finger prints. And make sure you don't splash anything off the plastic here okay? We don't want any DNA shit anywhere. Then we can wrap the rest of her up in this sheet and get it out to your pal at the booze-can there. Whattisname? Freddy?

Friendly.

That's the guy. Apparently he's got the right kind of re-moval system.

He does?

I saw it on that fucken show. That western. That town. Whattyacallit?

It's just a fucken farm.

The animals. That's what's important.

Pigs?

Exactly. They feed bodies to the pigs.

They do a good job?

Apparently they do a fucken terrific job.

Fucken eh huh?

What is the name of that show? It's going bug my head all day.

Was it on FOX?

No no. Some cable show.

HBO?

Quite likely.

Well like I said. I don't watch much TV myself.

No? What keeps you occupied most of the time?

Nothin. I don't mind. I like my deadtime.

Deadtime! Deadsomething. Deadfood. Deadman. *Dawn of the Dead*. Something like that.

Well. *DoubtShake*. Good luck gettin Friendly workin for ya. All he's good for is choppin wood.

Deadwood! How approfuckingpo.

Afternoon; hulk compound: GuardShift

MonsterPound chiefLair.

My man. Sit.

What's up?

Relax kid. Drink?

Guess so.

I got some twenty-one-year-old scotch.

Just a beer's good.

Gort baby. *CanHand.* When you gonna get used to your place in this world?

I'm fine. *SquirmShift leatherSqueak.* I'm used to my place.

You're not getting me. I need you to be confident. I need you to be in command.

Command. *Kaspoit!*

As in ready to run this place.

The boozecan? *SwillGulp.*

You already run the boozecan. I mean this place. All of it. Buildings. Vehicles. Businesses. Personnel. Connections. Security. Et cetera.

A promotion?

What else would it sound like?

What're you gonna be doin?

East. First of all. Gotta do some politicking back there.

How long?

That's just it. Not sure. That's why I'm fixing you up first. Even when I get back I'm gonna need a ready hand.

What about the other guys?

Look around.

Yeah?

What other guys?

I donno.

Geekster? He's fine with the clubs and dancing girls. Runs the coke fine. I don't want that touched. Get me? He's fine there and I don't want that touched.

Okay.

Scroaty?

Yeah maybe.

Too dense. By far. You see it. That coke bust through the border. He's a major heatbag now and from what I've seen he hardly even knows it.

I thought that was looked after.

What? The court bitch? Hah. Postponement. At most. Time enough for us to move his operation. He'll still have to show up and get a little time in the joint. In fact it's because of him I'm making sure you got a hold on things before I go. Have we moved him?

End of the week.

You got those busses?

Yup. Scroat apparently pulled some kinda thing with these Central American greasebacks who buy em for public transport down there. Let em buy em and then sidedealed em back to us for a coupla bucks commission. That way there's no auction records on us about who bought what.

Nice. Now get em buried on the new plot and let's restart this grow pronto. You got the excavators?

They're on Scroaty's place right now. Coverin up the breather vents.

Okay. When you're finished get em back to the rental outfit ASAP. It's money just sittin there.

Gotcha.

And make sure Scroat moves off that heatpad and gets a quick sale going. Get his bohunk family name right the hell off it.

In the works.

Is he going back with that bitch of his?

Gonna try I guess.

Well whatever he does he's gotta get a place in town out of the damn spotlight for a good long effen time. I'm getting sicka guys calling legal attention to themselves. It's hard enough keeping the cops in doughnuts without having to go hat-in-hand to these fuckers and try to keep my personnel out of the can. The debts I have to incur. The markers I have to pull in.

Sounds fucked up all right.

That reminds me. *FileDrawer.* Here. *CrossTable paperToss.* This is something important.

What is it?

It's got a seal on it. See? Don't open it til I tell you to.

Fucken mysterious Roberto.

Hafta be. It's enough to get anybody on the planet killed if they knew what was in it.

Jeeze.

And well the fuck you should say.

What am I sposed to do with it?

Hold onto it. Don't look at it. I'll be able to tell if you do. Try to forget it. But if anything happens to me it's something that might help out. No guarantees.

What the fuck's goin on?

Heavy shit caballero and the less you know about it the better your chances of seeing next year. Get me?

Fuck.

Well you might say. Now if all goes well back east some of this shit is going to simmer down. But I need you to keep things together while I'm gone.

I donno.

What don't you know?

If I wanna.

BurnStare. You think you got a choice?

Huh. It's that way is it?

What other way would it be?

This is some fucken shit.

Put it any way you like. Then get your ass in motion.

Nobody else can do this?

Nobody else.

SwillGulp.

HeavyQuiet.

CanSwill.

GulpMonster.

Want another one?

CanSwill. Naw.

Smart.

Guess I'll take a piss and get goin.

Good plan.

VetteGlide.

HulkPeer.

WindShield reInstall glueBulb. Fuck! *HulkSnarl fingerRun.*

GaragePark.

StompWalk.

StillKitchen.

BlareTV. StompWalk.

FemmeWatch. FurrowBrow upLook. That fucking kid of yours.

Is he why yer not in that kitchen cookin up sumpm?

Food is the last thing on my mind.

What the fuck now?

Reinhart's downstairs with some girl.

Huh. What's wrong with that?

He's using the Artemis lead crystal goblets. The rilly good ones.

What?

He's having a private party or something. I couldn't see all he's doing because he yelled at me when I went down there. But there's champagne missing and the good crystal and we don't even know this girl. I'm so pissed off.

Huh. *HulkGlance barrenKitchen*. So I guess there rilly isn't any chancea seein any kinda dinner anytime soon huh?

FemmeGlare.

Well I guess I'll go down and see what he's up to. She any good lookin?

How would I know? He's got her all bound up with duct tape.

Oh?

Some kind of fucking twisted critter you got there Gort. Congratulations.

Aw fuck.

BarWard beerFetch.

Kaspoit!

Better chug that thing and get another one. All you're good for around here these days.

Fuck off.

I mean what kind of parent are you anyway?

SwillGulp. I taught him a lesson the other day.

He obviously didn't learn anything.

HulkChug. CanToss.

For fuck sakes try to hit the garbage if you're too lazy to walk over there.

DownStair.

BassThrum.

RecRoom coolDark.

Anybody down here?

Dad. Stay the fuck away!

Not on yer fucken life. *LightSwitch.* Holy shit!

You always interfere.

Aw you fucken idiot. Why not have a straightahead date with a broad? Huh? Why not just take her out and get a meal and some booze in er and fucker later on. I don't even care if you knock some bitch up. But this. Whatter we gonna teller parents?

It's okay. She's an orphan.

Don't gimme that bullshit. Nobody's an orphan these days. Somewhere there's somebody that's responsible for her.

Well fuckem. That's what you always say.

Yeah yeah yeah. *ClosePeer*. Is she dead?

Think so. Stopped breathin anyway.

Well at least you gotter all wrapped up and ready to go.

Oh thanks a lot.

Shut yer fucken mouth.

I can't ever do anything right. Far as your concerned.

Well I rest my fucken case.

SideHead upSlap.

Ow!

RepeatStroke.

And that's for doin yer dirty shit in my house. What the fuck is in yer fucken sick mind?

TwoHand headSlap.

Ow.

Yer a complete fucken fuckup.

CanCrush headSore beerGush.

Ow!

Now getter down from there and clean up any sign of er and wrapper up and put er in the rear storage of the Navigator. Then before you get any supper you go over this whole fucken room with a mop and disinfectant. Then you stay out of my fucken sight while I figure out what the fuck we're gonna do to keep the school from comin over here and social services and the cops and the news media and every other fucken asshole who gets off on sex murder. See what kind of shit you get me into?

I'm sorry Dad.

Don't fucken cry. That's even worse.

Evening; parking lot: DickZap

MudEdge parkLot.
HulkHauler parkStop.
Hey you guys.
DuoMonster.
Hey. Gort is it?
Yeah. The other night. The fire.
Oh I didn't recognize you in daylight. Scroaty's your pal right?
Uh huh. How you guys doin? Gettin all yer work done that Roberto put ya to?
No need to ask.
Forget I did.
All you gotta know.
All I wanna fucken know. *HulkPull hatchBack.* You guys comfy here? *ShuckShirt.* Anything you want? *LeatherPull.*
Hey we're happy as shit.
Whener ya headin back?
Donno.
Fucken fine with us. Make yerselfs at home.
We got stuff to still do. *KillerPull hatchBack.* Couple more assignments for your man Friendly here.
Whoa. *HulkGlance.* I won't ask.
Yer a smart man. So that's why Roberto left you in charge.
You guys know about that?
Got our orders. Anything you want. We do.
All right then.
Got anything you want?
Lemme see. Oh yeah. I order you guys to go in the booze-can over there. Get some beer. Get some hookers. And drink and fuck yourselfs stupid all night.

Yes sir.

Uh huh.

TrekMonster.

ChokeSome liquorHole.

Kaspoit! miniSymphony.

Hey there he is now.

Fuck. I told Friendly to stay out of the bar. He stinks. Stew. Why is Friendly in here?

Hey Friendly. Get out yer wheelbarrow. Starve out your pigs. Sharpen up yer hatchet. We got a couple more for ya.

Aw heck. *DownCast.* Are you guys for real?

Friendly. Do as yer told.

Aw cmon Gort. You gotta see the bodycount these fuckers are rackin up. Just this mornin another one.

For the record Sport. *KillSneer.* That one was cold when we went to fuck her.

What?

Another onea the hookers looks like she OD'd last night. They made me get rid of er.

What do you mean another?

Well there was that one Scroaty fucked to death. Nobody knows rilly why she kicked off. Mighta been a OD. Then there was the business one they brought in all sliced up. Now you guys got two more?

Boys this time.

And who were these fellas then?

Hey Gort. *KillGrave.* You let the help do interrogations around here?

Shut the fuck up Friendly and do as these guys say. No questions. They tell you to get rid of a fucken elephant you go ahead and start renderin. Hear?

Whatever.

Besides. I got one for ya too.

Aw no.

The Navigator. Rear storage. Go scoop it out and get rid of it. Right now.

What's goin on around this crazy place?

There you go with those fucken questions again. Watch yerself. You wanna be the planter or the plantee?

Oh I figger I'm purty secure. Who else wouldya get to do away with yer problems? *OffStomp.*

Kaspoit! CanLift. Good point. *GroupYuck.*

SwillGulp. Effen eh.

Stunfuck moanernerd.

Yeah somethin like that. Hey Stew. What's the deal with your brother there? All this backtalk never been worse since we first took over this forsaken shithole.

It's perspective Gort.

Perspective?

He doesn't have any.

Why not?

Ever since he was a kid he's lived like this minute is the only one that exists.

Oh yeah?

Is that bad? *KillGrin.* I read a book once that said you should always be where you are. Or pick a spot and stick on it. Or stop thinking and just hum. Or something like that.

You read a book?

C'mon Flame. You seen me read.

A skinmag on the plane.

I got at least ten pages into it. Some bitch had it and give it to me.

The clap yeah.

The book fuckhead.

Anyways Stew. Perspective. I had a talk with him and he seems to think he's got a choice about what he does around here. Plain stark crazy. Not like you.

Naw. Not like me.

So what's up?

I donno. He was never okay. Always been scrambled. Just hung on rilly. Settled down acceptably once he discovered The Bible et cetera. But that's the only thing that seemed to help him.

The Bible?

Yeah. Only thing he ever read. Or had read to him. Not sure if he actually can read.

It would surprise the hell outta me. Was he always so fucked up?

Mom was drinkin pretty heavy when she carried him. Then she dropped him on his head. Then she fed him beer when he was a week old. Then she made him live in the pigshed when he was five. Then they kicked him outta school cause he stunk so bad. The rest is rock 'n' roll history as they say.

HulkGuffaw.

ChortleSnork.

What a fucken crew!

Well I gotta say that explains a lot!

So there you go. The guy's handicapped. No thinking ahead. No learning from experience.

Whatever happened to your good ol mom?

Somebody killed er. Nobody knows who.

Fuck. No offense but I'm glad to hear it. You and Friendly and your sister are a threeheaded bitch to deal with already.

Yeah well. We're nothin compared to her. You'd be fucken flummoxed man. She was hardassed.

Fuckit Gort. *HandSlap hulkBack.* You got some place here. Me an Chico are havin a blast. We got nothin like this back east.

No?

Hell no. I mean sure. We get together at some guys' places. Have a few beers. But it's all planned out and the city boozecans are fun but you can't horse around outside like you can here. I mean here you got fire always going. Booze always flowing. You got Stew here with his giant foodpot back of the bar. You got girls coming and going on regular rotation. Budget style hotel accommodation. *EyeWink*. Expert trash removal services. And all of it safe from prying straightjohn eyes. If I had a hat on man I'd take it off to ya.

Well glad you like the facility.

We more than like it. We heartily recommend the crazy place. We're puttin the word out man.

Yeah look. About that. We're pretty much up to capacity around here eh.

Aw it's not too crowded. The more the weirder.

Yeah okay but keep it down awright? The town's gettin closer and closer every time I look. Real estate is fucken sky-high. They're buildin townhouses within sight of the fire. Pretty soon we're gonna get noise complaints for fucksakes.

Sufferin shitbag mofo. *HulkSmirk*. You guys are lucky you don't got jailhouse complaints. If this place was ten klicks southa here the ATF FBI DEA and every other cop agency of the U.S.A. alphabet would be surrounding this place and plugging every asshole on the property with highgrade munitions.

Yeah well. We doen want anything like that.

Effen eh you don't. You got a real resource here. A classic case of Canadian limpass policing advantage. You guys should be floggin the shit out of it.

We doen wanna attract attention.

But there's money to be made Gort.

Yeah okay Chico. I'll put it on the lista things I gotta fucken do. *SwillGulp*.

But seriously you guys got it good here. You got the cops under control pretty good.

So far.

Nothin like back east. We're glad to be outta there.

Oh yeah?

Fucken rats everywhere you turn. Guys rolling over to get rid of parking tickets. Can't trust anybody. They're throwing guys to the cops every other week to keep the gang unit away from the door. They passed that special law in Quebec. The cops are starting to pack MiniMAC 10's and shooting first and asking questions never. It's fucken madness man. Be glad you're out here enjoying the BC fresh air.

No kiddin. That bad eh?

It's bad man.

So fucken bad we never want to go back there.

Huh.

So darn bad we don't care if we ever do.

Huh.

That's what Flame was saying. Weren't you Flame?

Damn right I was.

Might as well hunker down here as anyplace else.

What? You mean in the trailers?

Sure.

You guys like it in there?

Yeah.

Don't the hookers bother ya?

We screw the hookers. What's to bother?

Yeah but. You can't always be fuckin. You gotta get some sleep sometime dontcha?

Savage dickslam man. We ram em all night.

What about when they're fucken somebody else?

We listen in and laugh like crazy assholes.

Oh man. You guys are more haywire than anybody thought.

But in a good way. Right?

Ha ha ha.

Hey you're a fucken good guy Gort. Just call me Klaatu.

You fucken guys. I gotta take a piss.

Hey before you do that looky here. *PocketPull.* Take a boo at this little baby.

What the fuck is it?

Lemme take the cover off.

Issat a fucken Taser?

Rightyouare.

I thought you guys didn't fuck around in your work. Two to the chest and one to the head sorta stuff.

You got that effen precisely correct bud. This here's for fun. Me an Flame did some research. You know what happens when this bad boy zaps a body?

You shit.

Not so far. Not since we started using the thing. The opposite actually. You seize. All over. Then when the jolt cuts off you go limp and fall down. Theoretically.

Yeah. Thanks for that. Very educational.

Any time.

I hate fucken education.

Ha. Now just imagine what it's like when you got yer dick jammed as far up a bitch as it can go. Which. In Flame's case is . . .

Two feet.

Fuck off. Say ten inches.

What's that in metric?

Get fucken lost. So you got it up there and you give er a zap with this baby.

You electrocute your own cock. Brilliant.

Naw naw naw. There's a little twinge. A little spark. Kinda cool actually. You gotta keep your hands away. Let the current go through her and not you. So no ill effects. But up in the crack. The crack just goes apeshit man. The tension. The pressure. The pulse. The throb. I'm gettin a hardon just talkin about it.

Yer shittin me here.

Hey man. See for yourself. After we're finished with it.

Fuck Chico we're not ever gonna be finished with it.

Flame my man you said a crotchful baby.

You guys just go ahead. I'll take my sex action straight up if you don't mind. Sounds like the best reason for condoms I've heard since highschool. Thick ones.

Ewww.

Yeah yeah.

And buck tradition?

Yeah yeah.

Our boys go bareback or they don't go.

It's the code.

Onea the main reasons I'm in this crazy outfit.

Yeah yeah.

Besides. The brand of hooker you got around here. You gotta be a real man to fuck. Takes raw fucken courage. Where in hell do these bedbug hosebags come from anyway?

Downtown Eastside. Friendly and his sister round em up.

Can't you guys run better trade than this?

Sure we could but that's for makin money. We don't fuck the merchandize ourselves just like we don't toke the weed or blow the coke or crank the H or drop the E or do anything else the streetscuzz does. So you'll have to just fuck street whores or else get yourself a nice little woman and settle down.

Ewww.

Hey Gort. *BarHand phonePass.* Call for ya.

Here? Who the fuck is it?

Donno. Got this number though. So must know somebody.

Okay. I'll take it in the office. Is it clean in there?

Not too bad.

It better not stink like it did last time.

HulkStep.

CircumRoute drinkBrawl fistFest.

NicoSmoke cloudBank.

TalkDin.

DoorClose.

Yeah. Who's this?

Roberto.

Shit man. I just saw you yesterday.

A whole hell of a lot can happen in twenty four hours boy. Now listen up and listen good. I'm in a municipal joint somewhere near Saint Jerome.

What!

The harness bulls raided the house an hour ago. Got everybody.

Yer kiddin.

Yeah I do this kinda shit all the time. Just thought I'd call you up and fuck with your head.

Holy fuck.

Stop that shit and listen.

I can't fucken believe it.

Just let this go to show you fuckheads I protect out there how good you all got it. Not all jurisdictions have such a hold on the cops. Not everybody knows how to massage em into unconsciousness like I do.

What the fuck are we gonna do now?

Like I said. Yer gonna listen and do what I say. I need a million bucks.

What?

A million cash. In a hurry. At least a quarter of it right away. The rest in a month or so. We gotta get the best legal bodies around and we gotta start fightin this shit pronto.

Well. Okay. I guess I could go round and scrape up some cash out of the bodies we got here.

Yer the only free heads we got to turn to right now. All Quebec is under a court order. Ontario is half seized and the other half is scared shitless and not answering the goddamn phone.

How the fuck did it happen?

Aw they got this new law out here. Damned undemocratic if you ask me. We're gonna have to pull all the strings we got to make sure they don't pass anything like it out there.

Hey I guess you better not talk too much over the phone.

It's okay right now. I'm on the lawyer's mobile. In a private interview room. We called up the best guys we could find and they came right away. But they're gonna walk if they don't see long green by the end of the week. Apparently they been through this kinda shit before.

Fuck me.

Quit sayin fuck me and get your ass in motion Gort. I want out of this stinking lockup toot sweet.

Okay okay. Uh.

Uh what?

Where would you start lookin to scrape up the cash?

Go in everybody's poke. For starters. You and Geekster and Scroaty should be good for at least most of the down payment. Then you go through the membership and shake em for all you can. Then you mortgage the compound. We got at least three or four hundred G's in there. Sell all the extra cars and bikes. Quick like. And you mortgage whatever businesses you guys got that are making it. I know the ones. If anybody holds back they'll have my bootheels for eyesockets. And that's just for starters. Don't you guys forget that most of who they rounded up today could dick you guys and everybody else up real nice. So keep that in mind. You listening?

Uh huh.

Effen good.

I got you.

Any questions?

Naw.

Good. Get to it.

Hey what do you want me to do with those two killer fuck-heads they sent out?

Keep em. They'd just get busted here. Put em to work. They might come in handy.

Work? What fucken work have we got?

Well thinka somethin. Ol Papajohn is their pal out here. He raised em from pups. As long as they're happy he's happy.

They get him too?

Were you not listenin to me boy? I said they raided the place and they got everybody. Especially Papajohn. Mister big-time eastern megaboss. They got him trussed up in segrega-tion. It was him they were mostly after. The rest of us are just gravy. They don't even seem to know for sure who I am but that's bound to change awful damn fast. A lotta Papa's guys are quivering pussies. Put the squeeze on em and they'll start meowing all over the place.

Man.

Get me out!

I heard ya.

Good. Cause I gotta get off the phone.

Don't. *PhoneClick*. Worry.

FireSide.

JostleFest monsterBall.

HulkPiss arcSizzle.

Hey Scroaty.

Gort.

Seen Geekster?

Yeah. *Kaspoit!* Here somewheres.

Good. *FlyZip*. Tell him I gotta talk to him. And you too. Gimme a beer. Tomorrow. My place.

What's up?

JostleMonster. What the fuck's goin on?

Aw those eastern guys are jackin around.

ZapYelp. Aw fuck! *CrossFire downHulk.*

What the fuck!

Yeah. They're zappin guys with a Taser.

StumbleLurch yuckFest.

ZapShot monsterMirth.

And didya hear? They whacked Jerry and Shirt. My favourite fucken peons.

Oh. That was their names. I saw em bein offloaded.

Fuck man.

Well that Bellingham thing.

Yeah sure they fucked up. But they said they were sorry.

Hmmm. I guess Roberto figgered that wasn't good enough. And sent these two killcrazy fuckwads to do the job.

Yeah. *Kaspoit!* What a coupla fucken assholes.

Afternoon; living room: Cold-Shoot

Okay it's like this.

Kaspoit!

By now everybody knows the gang police back east did a big sweep. Nobody knows for sure what all they got in the way of evidence. Nobody knows if they'll make anybody do serious time. But the last time they did it they got a coupla top guys locked up for damn near life. So Papajohn might be gone for good. So who the fuck knows who's gonna be runnin things. And we might not be seeing Roberto for a fucken good long time either.

Kaspoit!

Well who gives a fuck about Papa? Only time we ever saw him was when he was through here on his way to Maui. Coppin a free fuck off my bitches.

Kaspoit!

And a free loada my weed.

And he'd hit up Roberto for some kind of equalization payola west supports east quote unquote cooperative mutual indemnity fuckwad fund. Least that's what Roberto used to call it.

They should raise their own fucken legal throw money.

I especially don't get this million dollar thing Gort. I mean. We have to take everything down? Stop production? Sell everything off for peanuts? And what for? The loss is way outsized for the so-called benefit.

Hey hey hey. You guys. You don't have to put up any arguments to me. Ever since I hung up the phone I been thinkin only about how we can gun this whole situation off. What we need is solid ideas. Scroaty. What's on your mind?

I don't fucken know. Only that I'm not gonna take down

my operation and go back to truck mechanicking for lousy union wages just because Roberto went and got himself scooped in some whorehouse bust back east. It don't add up.

Whattyou think Geek?

I say effen eh. Stop the profit line just because one of us gets in a jackpot? Fuck that. I say we take serious fucken action here.

Such as?

Why fuck around?

Off im?

Why not?

That was pretty much what I was thinkin.

I mean. Maybe you know the answer to this Gort. What are the real connections between us and them stupid Quebecois fuckers?

They more or less started the branch out here. Took it away from the slopes.

Yeah and we been havin Vietcong trouble every couplea years since. Some peacemaking Papa ever did.

Well we do operate in the open pretty much. Roberto calls it a protected environment.

For which we pay plenty. No?

Yeah I heard one time it was a shitload. One of the reasons Roberto likes to go back there himself. He hands em a suitcase fulla money and the party's on. Treat him like royalty.

Yeah well I say we take up our own protection and fuck those eastern bastards. We'd be a million bucks ahead the first year. Let em freeze in the dark.

I'm listenin Geek.

Good. 'Cause besides all that why do we care? I mean. The boozecan crowd won't. Would they?

Without Roberto they're just another buncha pimps and drug pushers. Standin around the fire pissing.

So replace Roberto with us. Simple.

Fuck stuff like that always sounds great when you say it but when you try to actually do it. Fuck.

We'd stand with ya Gort.

Thanks Scroaty. But I donno.

We might not have a choice. Stuff has to get done now.

You're right there. Scroaty's grow op being the biggest one. And the boozecan. Fuck. That needs straightenin out in the worst fucken way.

So I think we agree. Roberto's out. Without him we take over clean.

Okay then. Scroaty?

I agree.

Okay I'm with you guys. But we gotta stick together.

Effen eh.

I'm there man.

Good. So. How do we do it? Geek?

Why don't we just shoot ten grand to some junkie back there to gut him right in his cell? I'd spring for that.

I like that idea. Far away. And soon as possible.

Whoa now. We gotta think this thing through a little better. Who do they have to send after us?

By the sound of things back there they're too busy tryin to make bail to worry about what's goin on out here. At least for a good long time anyway. At least for as long as it'll take for us to grab a good hold on things and get ready for anythin they might try. And all Roberto's guys are here. And we're most of em. I mean. He hardly even knows who works for me.

Same here. He never even came and looked at my stuff. How bout you Gort?

We only ever met at the compound. With all those muscle-heads standin around.

Didn't he leave you in charge?

Yeah.

Well. Order em to get goin somewhere. Anywhere. Send em on a chore and cut off their cash. Put em to work doing somethin. Anythin. If any of em whine just whack em.

And that's another fucken thing. What about Chico and

Flame? They're the only real connection we got to all this shit back east.

Did you see those fucken idiots last night? They killed another hooker I heard. With that dumb fucken zapper thinga theirs. Even fucken Stew is startinta complain about em. Hangin around all the time. Drinkin for free. They're gettin to be a real fucken paira pests.

To put this eastern thing further away from us we gotta do somethin about these guys right fucken now.

Whack em?

What else?

I don't see nothin else. They got attitude. Think they're hot as freshly squeezed shit. Likely still think they got truck with the eastern guys.

Anybody told em about the bust?

They gotta know somehow.

If not now soon. And I wonder what they'll be like when they realize they're workin without a net.

Might get fucken dangerous.

You got a fucken good point Geek. These guys operate with total sanction from Papajohn and whoever else it is pulls the fucken strings back east. When they find out they're on their own fuck knows what they'll try to do.

Maybe try to take us over.

Why not? They see we're mostly business and party types. They're the killers.

Aw we gotta have somebody who can take out the trash. What about Rudy?

Didntcha hear? They killed fucken Rudy. Along with a carloada fucken ruckmumps last month just after they landed.

What! I liked ol Rudy. Crazy fucker but he knew his guns.

Yeah but ya kinda knew he was bound for shit sooner or later. I mean he was sellin to kids by the end. Cops had him dead to rights. He was hotter than one of his own cheap pistols. Roberto never shoulda sent those guys to him for their

gun supply. We coulda done just as good outta Friendly's
toolshed.

You think Roberto was kinda losin it?

If you step back and take a look at the thing. All that's happened for the past coupla years. You might say so.

Fuck Gort it's been obvious for a long fucken time. You take
away our ops and what's he got? The boozecan? Guys are hardly
botherin to pay their dues anymore. Total lack of discipline.
And I think Stew is cookin the books too. Shortin the bottom
line left and right. Not that that shithole would ever make a guy
a decent living anyway.

Whateverthefuck. Nevemind all that shit. What we gotta do
now is make up our minds about what we're gonna do and go
ahead and do it. Ourselves. No hired hands.

Whattya sayin?

Dust off yer guns.

Aw I haven't killed anybody in like ten years.

That's just my fucken point. We've gone soft.

I'm ready. Got my nine with me right now.

That's another thing. Those psychos are gonna bump hip to
this thing any second if they haven't already. They'll get awful
damn jumpy awful fucken fast. Everybody pack heat from
now on until we got this thing done.

Let's whack those motherfuckers today.

That's what I got in mind. How bout you Scroat?

I gotta go take a piss. But if you guys say it's gotta be done
then I guess it's gotta be done.

Second door on the right. Don't piss on the floor. And hey.
A little more enthusiasm okay? This is life and death shit
here. We gotta seize the fucken day.

Whatever you say Gort. *RiseHulk*. I guess that's why
Roberto left you in charge. *HallRumble*.

Hey I didn't ask for this. He pushed it on me. Fuck knows
why.

Couldn't handle it himself anymore. Soft in the fucken head.

Right on.
Just another example of why we should cut him loose.
Okay. Glad you can see my side of it.
Hey Gort. We gotta stick together.
Glad you see that too.
We're fucked on our own. Side by side we're bitchin.
That's the way it always seems to go.
Right on.
But keep this dead quiet.
HulkZip slumpCouch.
Hear that Scroaty? Mum's the fucken word. Not even your old ladies. Meet at Friendly's tonight. Bring heat.
UniGrim canTilt.
Okay I guess that's enough yakkin.'
Anybody got a question?
Nope.
Nope.
RiseHulk. Let's get to it.
Right you effen are Gort.
FileMonster.
HulkDoor. Seeya round ten.
Gotcha.
Right.
BrickPath monsterWalk.
BrowFurrow stepPace purseLady.
SideStep fileHulk.
Mister Brownbeck.
HulkBack doorClose.
ThroughDoor. Mister Gordon Brownbeck? *DoorHammer.*
FurrowThink. Mr. Brownbeck I must speak with you. About a missing girl!
DoorCrack. Uh. What's the deal here?
You are Gordon Brownbeck?
I never answer questions from strangers.
I'm Gloria Jorgenson. Shanelle Bolger's guardian.

Uh.

Your son. Reinhart? Shanelle is his girlfriend.

Uh.

They said at the school she was your son's girlfriend.

They told you this address?

Well not exactly. They told me they couldn't tell me where Reinhart lived. Privacy rights or something like that. I had to kind of steal it off the secretary's computer. I was just sitting there waiting for the principal and she went out of the office. And of course as you know you're not listed in the directories. But I'm sure you're okay with my just asking if you've seen Shanelle or know where she might be.

HulkScan streetScape. Where'd you park your car?

I'm on the bus. And walking. I guess you must drive all the time. The stop is a long way off from here.

DoorWide. Come in.

Thank you.

HulkLead downStair.

I'll admit she's run away before but I always found her. Usually with some boy or other. Poor thing is starved for love and oh so low in the self-esteem department.

Uh huh.

She's been with me since she was dumped in my lap by my nogood cousin. God knows where that poor hopeless drug addict might be. Dropped little Shanelle off with me when she was three. It hasn't been easy I'll tell you that for sure. She's a good kid really but you know. Trouble with drugs. Served some juvie time last fall. But she was doing fine in school she showed me her marks. But now this. And she was just turning her life around.

Uh huh.

EyeWide lookAround. My what a humongous house. Your basement looks as big as the whole floor of our apartment building.

Uh huh. *PolySpread.*

Oh are you doing some kind of home project? It must be nice to have such a lot of time on your hands.

Uh could you just stand here for a sec.

On the plastic?

Yeah.

Do you need help covering something up or something?

Just stand there for a second.

Well okay. If it'll help find out where Shanelle might have got to.

DrawerShuffle. Just stand right there a sec.

Have you lost something? *BackStare.* Can I help you find it? *PistolWheel.*

PointClose blankRange. NineRound chestHole.

Oh. *FemmeKnee downBuckle.* Oh. *NineBullet headPunch. BackFall downBody.*

Night; mobile home: FiendFight

Geez Friendly. Looks like you cleaned the place up. What's goin on?

Wasn't me. My friend Maisie. She likes it a little more tidy.

You should keep her around.

She's my pal. We used to play in the sandbox together.

No kiddin. You got friends?

Acourse I got friends. Whattyou tryin ta say Gort?

Nothin. I got no time to shoot shit with anybody anyway. I'd siddown but I don't like the looka that sofa.

It's okay since we fumigated.

Nevermind. We can stand and talk bizness.

What bizness?

Whereabouts are those two eastern guys?

Flame and Chico? In the boozecan last I saw.

Fuck it's only two in the afternoon. You sure?

They start in early and don't hardly do nothin else.

What time they usually go to the hooker trailer?

The hooker trailer? How should I know when they go to the hooker trailer?

I thought I told you to know everything that goes on here.

Why you wanna know when they go in the hooker trailer? You plannin a surprise party?

You could say that. But the less you know the better.

Well it's gotta be around eleven or midnight.

Okay tonight I want you to keep an eye on em and let me and Scroaty and Geekster know when they go in. Okay?

If you say so.

And don't talk about this. Don't mention it to anybody.

Don't talk about what? I got plentya stuff to do already.

Oh yeah. That reminds me. I got another stiff in the Navigator fer ya.

What?

You heard me.

Whatter you fellas up to these days? I mean. We never had no need for body removal like this in the old days.

Old days? When were the old days?

Um. Well. Before a few months ago.

Yeah the good old days a few months ago. They'll come back again. We just gotta deal with some shit and maybe we'll have the good old days back with us right quick. Hang in.

I sure hope so.

Amble Hulk.

Dusk Light site Survey.

Access Egress.

Sex Window measure Look.

Booze Can. Duo Monster bar Lean.

Hey you guys. *Hulk Lean.* When you get here?

Just now.

See the killers?

Naw. Stew said they went to get some food. Got tireda his stewpot morn likely.

Where's Stew?

He went to get a cratea booze or somethin. Said these beers we're drinkin are the last ones.

Fucken typical. At least we got the place to ourselves for a sec.

What's up boss?

I looked over the layout. Unless you guys got other strategies I guess the best would be to coincide our shootin with their fucking.

Sounds sensible.

Apparently they cofuck. One bitch at a time. In the same room.

How do we know this?

The bitch I did last night was with them the night before. That's what she said.

Hmm.

They go at it from midnight through to around four. Two or three girls.

Somebody sellem Viagra?

Oh they eat plenty of that stuff. And Cialis too and any other kinda dick stiffener. Grind it up and crank the shit apparently.

Naw fuck.

Yer kiddin.

What I heard.

Real fuckers in the truest sense I guess.

Whatever the effen hell. I'm just concerned with gettin em outta the fucken pitjure permanently.

A-fuckenmen ta that.

So here's our advantage. We're gonna be stone sober. Right?

Acourse.

You got it.

And they'll have been drinkin for twelve or fourteen fucken hours. And doin whatever other shit. And busy dickin. We should get the drop on em.

How you wanna play it?

I figger two guys at the door. One at the window. The guys inside kicker down and start blastin. That's the signal for the guy outside to fire away. And don't just give em two pops each and stand down. Empty your rods into em and reload if you have to and don't stop until they're leaked out and done twitchin.

Okay.

Should we do the wooden stake through the heart?

Fucken funny.

Sounds like we're gonna fucken massacre these fuckers.

You thought up any other way?
Nope.
Okay then. Everybody got their steel?
Yup.
Vests?
We need em?
You never know.
Mine's in the car.
Good. By the way. You each owe me thirtythree hundred and thirtythree.
Yeah?
Got through to my Montreal guy. Gonna take cara Roberto. He's in a lockup where people go in and out easy. He'll be a deadman by morning.
Effen eh deadman. That'll be a fucken relief. You work fast Gort.
Somebody's gotta take the fucken initiative around this slackass place.
Well you da man. What's our move after?
Lotsa shit. I'm workin on it. First things first.
Effen eh. When do we go?
I'll give the word. Quit drinkin. Everybody take a good long piss. Don't go too far away.

NightDark fireShadow.
Ain't it about fucken time?
Steady there boy.
Fuck it Geek. I put off heavy beerin for this. When's we gonna get to it?
Gort said when he said. Just keep it warm.
I got it here against my gut.
Pointin at yer dick probly.
Mattera fact it is. That's why I keep the safety on.
Izzat Gort comin?
ShadowMonster. Hey you guys.

Hey.
Step away.
Field Huddle.
We set?
Yup. Who wants to take the window?
Who's got the heaviest gun?
I got my nine.
That's what I got.
I got a nine. Plus my trusty sixgun fortyfive.
Yeah?
Here it is.
Holy fuck it looks like a fucken negro hardon.
Got it years ago down in L.A. From an actual bad mother-
fucken negro in fact.
Then I guess it's you at the window Geek.
Okay.
Anybody bring anything automatic?
What you mean like an AK?
Yeah.
I got my Uzi in the trunk.
Loaded?
Always.
Good. You never know. I got onea these new 74s. Never
fired it but I assume it's a good gun.
Oh it's a fucken good gun all right but isn't the plan we
pistolero these bastards right in their hooker room and just
leave it at that?
That is exactly the plan but it's always good to have a
backup.
Okay.
These guys are professionals after all.
Gotcha.
And I don't know for a fact they don't wear their vests at all
fucken times. Get me?
For fuckin? They'd wear their vests fuckin?

Under all that leather who fucken knows for sure?
I guess.
Okay then. Let's rock.
Lock and fucken unload on em men.
Effen eh.
Hey Gort. Which window?
Oh yeah. The third one.
The third one on the door side or the non door side?
The door side. From the door. Third from the door. Watch out they don't see you.
Don't you fucken worry.

KillTrap hulkForce.
ClutchGun sneakStep.
HulkCannon windowPose.
SqueakFloor hallCreep.
GunPoint doorSwing.
What the fuck!
Fuck man. Sorry.
Get the fuck outta here.
Right the fuck away man.
DoorClose.
LipShush. Shit. *WhisperTone.* I thought I knew for fucken sure which room they're in.
Let's fucken hope Geek fucken figgers it out.
Let's just go find em. Geek'll get hip soon efuckennough.
HallCreep.
LaughCackle. FemmeSqueak.
TwoHand gunButt doorPush.
Whoa. *RoomCramp threeSome.*
HookerSplay.
HulkHandle zipHole jeanSprout KillerDick.
Fucken faggots! *HulkFire nineShot.*
HookerScream.
HulkFire. CacophoDin.

YellMonster angerFire. Scuzzy! *AngerFire.* Fucken! *AngerFire.*
Cocksuckin! *AngerFire.* Faggots! *FireFire.*

KillerReel. Why you makin us die?

FortyfiveShot glassHail.

FlashMuzzle strobeScape.

HulkFall sloMo strobeStage.

SpeedBullet thwockLeather.

TeeterKill gunGrapple.

AngerFire blindStrobe blastClamour.

KillerSquirm downFloor gunGrapple.

Cmon you fucken idiots! *AngerFrenzy hulkFire.* Die!

Effen fucken eh. *HulkCease scatterFire.* They're wearin
fucken vests. *ReAim.* Headshots!

ClickMonster. I'm outta fucken ammo.

FireAcrid screenSmoke fogThick.

GunGlint floorBase.

Back off he's gonna start shootin!

OffFloor nineBlast.

MonsterLurch.

SleeveGrab pullHulk.

BlunderBlast windowShower fireCover.

StumbleRun.

DuoMonster rumbleDark stumbleFlee.

WoodBound struggleRun.

RunStop breathCatch.

HulkStomp twoHand pistolGrip.

Hey you guys. *WoodRustle hulkRampage.*

Geek! Over here.

What the. *WheezeBreath.* Fuck happened?

They had their. *HackCough.*Vests on. *GaspHulk.* They fuck
wearin. Their fucken kevlar.

GroundFlat groanMonster.

How bad are ya Scroat?

He took at least one.

My shoulder.

Just hold a hand to it an squeeze.

Whatter we gonna do? Are they dead?

Donno. I could hardly aim the smoke was so bad.

All I saw was the flashes. It was the wrong window so I had to hustle. Then started blastin. Did I hit em?

They both went down but I don't think they're dead. Chico got the round off that hit Scroaty. I think.

Guess we better get the rifles.

Fucken right. They'll try to get to their car.

We can get em comin off the garbage mound. The only way they'd go in the dark.

We better fucken hope.

You gonna be okay here Scroaty?

Help me up. I gotta get a drink.

Water?

Fuck that.

Boozecan's that way.

I know where the fucken boozecan is. *TotterHulk*. Get them dickpullen faggots. I'm gonna drink me a river. Get that faggoty jerkoff pitjure outta my head.

BleedHulk lurchWalk.

DuoMonster parkLot trotRun.

WaifLair.

Oh you kept it nice!

Course. I wouldn't dirty up all yer good work.

And you showered and shaved and put on a clean set of clothes. Much better than that day in the mall.

Well I wanted to at least smell better.

That was very considerate of you Frederick.

Aw stop it. No big deal.

Well considering what it was like in here before. I'm surprised it wasn't condemned.

Hah. Nobody ever comes here. How could it get condemned?

That's right isn't it. No one ever comes to see you.

Nope.

And if it hadn't been for our chance meeting at the mall we'd never have linked up again would we?

Doubt it.

Don't you ever go to town and get supplies?

Every so often, but mostly Rosa does that.

Your sister. I never knew her very well.

Yeah I guess she was a bit too far ahead of us in school.

And you didn't have such a good relationship with her as I remember. Your mother was kind of difficult too if I recall.

Yup we were quite the wild bunch back then.

Well things seem reasonably fine now. You have your cozy little trailer. Do Stew and Rosa live on the farm too?

Naw they got a house in PoCo. They come purt near every day though. Rosa keeps the groceries comin. Stew does odd jobs.

And you?

I do the actual farmin.

You still farm?

One pig. All that's left. I got a big garden though.

And cats and dogs I suppose.

Well cats anyway. We usedta have a dog. Gotta get another one.

Oh. Well. Should we sit down?

Sure sure. You want a drinka sumpm?

Sure.

I got beer.

Oh. I didn't know you were drinking alcohol these days.

I don't. I like these jumbo size bottlesa cola. My brother keeps all the booze over in the big shed. I can get wine or whisky for ya if you'd like.

I'd be perfectly happy with a cup of tea. Or whatever you're having.

I can make tea. *WaifShift.*

That would be lovely but.

KitchenLoud potClang. What?

Don't go to any trouble.

Huh?

I said don't go to any trouble! It sounds like you're taking the place apart!

I know I got a tea pot here somewheres. Rosa gave me one for my birthday about ten years ago.

Well if you can find it that would be great. But really you just need two cups and a kettle.

Yeah that's how I usually do it.

Well then maybe I can help. Have you looked above the stove?

Nope. I gotta get a stepladder.

I wish you wouldn't go to such lengths.

I'm gonna go whatever length I gotta go to make you feel at home Maisie.

FrontRoom couchSit.

Lovely tea.

Glad you like it.

And you got these cute little animal crackers we had when we were kids.

Thought you'd like em.

You're so nice Frederick. That's what I remember. How did we lose touch for so long?

Oh I guess I had to wander.

Yes that's what you said that afternoon you told me you weren't coming to school anymore. Grade Ten.

Yeah somewheres around there.

You left school and I never saw you again except in the papers occasionally. Your family had some kind of fight with the municipality.

Yeah I remember that.

And then the animal control raid back in the late eighties.

Yeah they thought we were mistreatin the livestock.

The way I read it it sounded like the developers were trying to get your stinky farm moved right off the countryside. However did you win that one?

Well we had to reduce. Used to raise a good two three hunnert swine a year on the place. Nowadays it's more just a hobby.

And the fancy cars I see parked around that paved spot by the barn?

Yeah we sell space for auto storage. I also got a wreckin business.

Oh? I didn't see that.

Yeah I got a good few hunert wrecks over past the feed shed there. In the gully. You can't see em from anywhere on the road or anything. But it's not a bad little business.

So I suppose that's how you've kept things going all these years since your mom's passing? Without actually going out and getting a wage earning job.

Yup.. You got it. I been lucky.

Well I'm sure you worked hard. At least your brother and sister got away and established themselves off the property. Did you ever leave like you said you were going to?

Yeah I traveled around a bit. Didn't like it though.

No?

Nope.

Where all did you go?

Oh Toronto.

Just Toronto?

Yeah.

And you didn't like it?

Nope.

Too big?

I'll say.

Didn't you make any friends?

Only stayed three days. Got lost a lot. Just barely made it out of there with enough money for the train.

Oh you took the train across the country. I've always wanted to do that.

Well goin out was okay. I had money and a little room to sleep in.

The scenery must be wonderful.

Yeah I guess.

I've only ever seen it from the air. Several times. And once from a car window when I was little.

Well comin back I saw a lot of it cause I had to sit up. Fer four days. With nothin ta eat.

Oh my. Quite an adventure.

Never wanna do that again.

No. Being poor is no fun.

We always been poor. Sort of. But I never had a time I couldn't get somthin ta eat.

It would be a trauma to most of us I'm sure.

A what?

A trauma.

What's that?

A trying time. A bad surprise. An upsetting shock that makes you tremble and have nightmares.

Well that was what it was like all right.

I've been getting by on nearly nothing myself.

Not you Maisie. I thought your family was rich.

Compared to yours perhaps. But daddy died when he was only fifty-three and his business hadn't been doing that well. Mother had to go out nursing again and she hated it. I never got to university as I had yearned to do. So sad. Ha ha I'm always feeling sorry for myself.

Well it is kinda sad.

No matter. I eventually took a business admin certificate at Kwantlen College and worked for the federal government.

Them's good payin jobs.

Yes if you can stay in them. I had to take a disability leave.

Were you hurt?

Inside. I was hurt inside Frederick.

Gosh.

I knew you'd understand. Would you like to come sit beside me?

Well sure. I guess.

Ragged Sidle.

That's better.

Did you take some medicine? Are you better now?

For what? Oh my hurt inside. Yes. You might say I did.

I never been to a doctor my whole life.

Really? No. You must have at some time. For vaccinations at least.

At school I remember. But nothin after that. I was just never sick.

Living amongst the animals. All that dirt. I suppose you must have built up a resistance.

Yeah maybe somethin like that.

Well I never had a resistance. I was weak inside.

You were?

Don't you remember me as a young girl?

I do. You were sweet and nice. Not like the other kids.

Thank you for remembering.

Just like now. You're still sweet and kind. Pretty too.

We'll I appreciate your admiration. I try to keep myself fit.

You're thin as a snake.

Well certain illicit chemical agents can do that for you.

Illiciwhat?

Frederick can we be sweetly honest with each other?

Aw gee that'd be great.

I'm not as pure as you seem to like to idealize me as. I've had some hard knocks.

Who did it? I'll go after em for ya if ya want me to.

No no no. Nothing like that. The fact is that for every hard knock I got I knocked right back. Don't worry. And I found refuge.

Refuge? Like a house or somethin?

In drugs.

Oh.

Nothing terribly nasty. Just a little cocaine.

Yeah?

There was a crack episode. I'm not proud of it.

I heard that stuff rots yer brain.

I can testify as to the veracity of that statement.

SmileyLaugh. Yer funny.

About what?

Yer rassety word. Ver rassety. Sounds funny.

Hah hah. You always were an easy room for the amateur standup. You do a girl's ego good.

I'm glad fer that. Don't know how much else I can do.

Oh Frederick you have a worker's muscles. Let me feel them. ·

Sure.

Wrap them all around me.

Okay.

I used to dream about this when we were kids.

What. Sittin around talkin?

Touching Frederick. Talking and touching and being together.

Gee. I never knew you felt that way Maisie. I always liked
you a lot though.

That's good. So much time has passed.

That's fer sure.

Kiss me.

Huh?

Mmmmm. *Mouth Buss.*

Whoa.

What's wrong?

Nobody ever did that before.

Kiss?

With yer tongue like that.

No?

I liked it though.

You've never done that?

Nope.

Frederick. Are you a virgin?

What's that?

A person who's never had sex.

Well I guess I am then. I figger.

You're not sure?

Well I don't know. I kinda don't know a lot in that department.

Does it embarrass you to talk about it?

Kinda. I don't usually talk like this. With anybody. With you
it's all right though.

Really?

I always rilly liked ya.

That's so sweet.

Nothin perticalarly sweet about it. Just fact that's all.

So you've never loved a woman?

Well it depends on what you say love is kinda. I mean. Deep feelings.

Well. I've kinda deeply liked somea the girls they get for the fellas around here. They're sometimes nice to me. They suck at me with their mouths. If I clean up good that is.

Oh. So you do have some experience.

But not so's you'd say they loved me or nothin.

Uh huh. I see what you mean. I'm glad you draw the distinction.

You are?

Of course. So many men get fixated on the physical part of love. That's all it is to them sometimes. They forget about the heart and the brain. All they think about is their dicks.

Oh. Well. I'm not that way.

I can see that.

Good.

And it's damn sexy.

What is?

The fact you don't just want to roll a girl in the hay and walk away and not think about love. That's a wonderful attribute in a man.

Gee. Yer sure buildin me up here.

Well it's not hard to do. I'm just delighted to find that after all these years the sweet boy I remembered has grown up to be a sweet man.

I wish everbody thought that way.

Oh. Don't you get along with other people?

Mostly. But some of the kinda guys who hang around this place are sure nasty sometimes. They make me do awful things.

Really? What kind of awful things.

Oh just cleanin up their messes. They make an awful mess sometimes.

What kind of a club or hangout or social society thing do

they run here? You mentioned there was a number of regular types who hang around.

Yeah it's kind of a business association. That's what one of em said it was one time. Mostly they just stand around the bonfire and drink. Some of em sit around the boozecan and get pissed. A buncha them like to go and play with the gals in the hooker house.

Hooker house?

You know. Girls from town.

They have prostitutes from town come and stay in a special building?

You shouldn't ask no more questions about it Maisie. Nobody's sposedta know.

Oh. Okay.

Let's just stay in here and have a good time. You want another cuppa tea? Or a drink? I got lotsa little miniature booze bottles.

Would it bother you if I took a drink?

Oh no. I'm okay with it. I don't like booze no more so it's easy to stay off it. But you're morn welcome to have one.

Do you have any girl drinks?

Girl drinks?

Like Kahlua and cream or Crème de Menthe or Malibu or anything that smells like perfume.

Perfume?

Or suntan lotion or anything like that.

Suntan lotion! I got one that stinksa coconut.

That's a good one.

I'll pour ya one right now. *JumpRise*. Do ya take it straight or over ice or some other kinda way?

I think over ice would be fine.

LegStretch couchComfy.

ServeGlass. Here ya go.

Come here you fool.

Hey. Why you callin me a name?

Kidding silly.

Heh heh.

You are pretty foolish though. In a good way.

I'm glad.

It's lovely to be here with you.

You sure look comfortable.

You ain't seen nothin yet.

No?

That's a line from a movie.

I don't see too many movies.

No worries. Let me drink this drink. And sit down Freddy. I'll do the rest.

Aw gee. That's.

Popopopopopopbangbangbang.

Aw man.

Freddy! What is that?

Popopopopopopbangbangbang.

Stoopid ijeeits. *HeadShake.*

WarDin nearDistant.

Popopopopopopbangbangbang.

Aw it's those darned ijeeits shootin off their guns.

Popopopopopbangbang.

Don't the neighbours complain?

Popop. Bangbang.

They sure do.

GunPause.

My god.

Yeah sometimes it sounds pretty bad.

I'd say it sounds like a massacre going on.

Naw they just play around.

Well I'm glad it's not right next door. But it sure sounds scary.

Yeah. *WaifSigh.* Gee Maisie. I think I gotta go and check to make sure things are okay.

You mean over there? Toward the shooting?

Yeah.

Are you sure it's safe?

I just gotta go and tell em to stop playin around.

Will they listen?

They better. The cops'll be here more'n likely.

And that's the sort of thing you take care of?

Uh huh. Sorta.

Will you be gone long?

No.

Well. Should I wait for you?

Wouldya? I'd sure like it.

Of course I will. If you promise to hurry back.

Ragged Stir. I sure hate to get up off this couch with ya Maisie.

What a sweet compliment.

Too bad I gotta go do what I gotta do.

Night; hooker stall: SideSwipe

GunSmog coughChoke.
HandWave.
DarkBlind pistolAim.
Flame. *PhlegmHack.* You alive?
Yeah. Pretty sure.
Where?
LoomMonster. Right here. *KneeLift bootBed.* I'm pulling my
backup.
Good. I think I can get up.
Where you hit?
Arm. They winged me fucken good.
Which arm?
Left.
Good. Your shooting shouldn't be affected.
You fucken kiddin? *HackCough.* I can barely fucken
breathe. *StruggleRise.* My knees. Not sure I can walk.
Well you better get pretty damn nimble awful fucken fast
buddy. These guys aren't kidding around.
Yeah effen eh.
They took off scared though. I think you got one of em.
You think so?
We might have a second or two to reset.
I fucken hope so.
Fuck something hurts!
We gotta think this out. You hit?
Two in the leg. Grazed. I think they shot off a chunka my
ear.
When I breathe it's like fire. Think they punched me in the
chest about a hundred fucken times.

Got me in the back. Somebody was packing a fucken forty-five. Broken fucken ribs for sure.

Fucken alpha shitbag. What the fuck is goin on?

We shoulda took that news back east more serious.

We gotta think this out.

That's my fucken line. You used it twice now. Trying to take over my fucken role in this here partnership? Whattya think I'm doing here?

Sorry man. My fucken head is pounding. I can hardly hear. *WaverStand*. Ah my fucken arm. Hey. Where's the hooker?

She's here. On the bed. Shot to fucken shit.

Jeezusfuckenchrist they sure are hard on bitches around here.

You're not fucken kidding.

We did this back east we'd be fucked.

Not sure we're not fucked here as it is. They sure as hell gotta be laying for us outside.

They gonna come back and try it again?

Not likely. They know we're up and gunned. Good thing you got off a shot.

Yeah. Not sure where it went.

I heard that head guy. Gort something. Yelled the retreat. I think he was dragging the other guy.

I'm for going out and getting these fucken clowns *avec envoi*.

That'd be nice but let's look at this. They gotta have a backup plan.

You figger?

They're not the best assassins in the fucken world that's for sure.

We are.

Beside the point. We're shot up. They might be too but not near as bad. They seem to think it's a good idea to off us pair. Why? Sure as hell it has to do with that shit back east and somesuch total crapola thing going on around here. Most likely a Roberto-is-toast-so-let's-take-over type powermove among the leftover players. Taking over regional control. Cutting ties with the national boss. I'm trying to think what it was that Papajohn was saying to us.

He said somethin fucken funny. I'll never forget.

What was it?

Call the cops.

No. He was kidding.

You heard him.

I heard him but I thought he was kidding.

He said call the cops. If anything goes wonky. And he wasn't smiling. That's what I heard him say.

It was just a figure of speech.

Figure or not that's what he fucken said. You only halfheard it but I heard it fullon. I was listening real careful. He didn't say which police. Or who.

Naw this is no good to us right now. We gotta get outta here that's the only fucken sure thing.

How you figger it?

Haul out your backup. Two guns each. We plow straight outta here and make for the car. No telling how many of those assholes out by the fire might be in on it. We could have twenty guns on us. Thankfuckenchrist it's dark out.

There's plentya bushes and trees.

Right. Stay off the path.

I can barely hold this twentyfive. My arm.

Just wave it around and pull the trigger. More noise the better.

I guess so.

I know so. These fucken guys are scared.

MonsterDuo holdRise.

Fuck my leg hurts.

WallBounce.

I theen dats a good teeng. Means it's still working.

Fucken great. That must mean my back and my chest and

the left side of my face and my former earlobe is workin like a fucken charm too.

Okay get it together. *KillerGrip*. Lean on me.

We gotta blast outta this tin can and make for the dark. Away from those pathway lights.

Okay. Got your weapons ready?

Let's fucken go.

Let's fucken go.

DoorBurst.

ShambleRun threeLeg.

QuietFarm.

Wherethefuck. *RunGasp*. Arethey?

Think it through. *RunGasp*. Everybody heard the gunfire and they're staying the fuck away. *RunGasp*. Nobody wants any part of it. That means there's likely only the three in on it. That means we got a good chance. They know we'll go for the car. They're set up somewhere near sure as hell. *RunGasp*. We gotta be ready for em.

How's your leg?

Still working.

Hurts like hell eh?

Effen eh.

DuoStumble.

BushPlow stumbleDitch.

Fuck. Where's the lights? *HardBlink*. Can't see the parking lot.

If they cut the power and think they got an advantage they're fucked in the head.

BrightSavage gunFlash.

DirtFly.

DoubleFire defenseVolley.

GunLight.

CarHulk.

FireSqueeze doorPull.

PistolFusillade wildAim.

FumbleKey.
BulletRattle.
MotorRoar.
WindowPose pistolFire.
OneHand killerDrive wildShoot.
TireScreech.
MetalCrunch.
WheelFight wildShoot.
VelociFlee.
ShootShootShootShootShootShootClickClick.

Turn the fucken headlights on. I think we're away from the fuckers now.

Ya think?

There's the road!

Fuck!

WheelWhirl rubberScream.

That was fucken close.

What. You mean your driving or the fucken shootout we just survived?

Everyfuckenthing.

Yeah yeah.

Where the fuck am I goin?

Toward town. I think this is the way. Just keep driving. I gotta think this through.

We gotta get a medic on these dings we got.

Yeah yeah. I'm okay for now. How bout you?

I'm okay to drive to the nearest fucken hospital.

Naw naw. You know the procedure.

How the fuck do we know anything anymore? Papajohn's in jail.

He still left us with this phone number.

Yeah the phone number. Whatthefuck is all the secrecy about anyway? Can't tell you what it's for but don't lose it. Don't use it unless you absolutely have to. Just call the cops.

Fuck man. What was up with ol Papajohn anyway? How do we know he's not dead himself now or if not maybe it's him tryin to kill us?

We'll just have to find out for ourselves. Surely to hell we still got a play or two around here.

I wouldn't be too fucken sure.

Well I guess we better use the number.

Ya think?

This seems like an emergency.

Glad you think so.

We can't use the cell.

Course not.

Find a gasbar with a payphone. There's gotta be one left in the world.

OneArm killerCruise. JerkCareer curbSwipe.

Fuck. *GrimFace.* We'll be lucky if the cops don't get us for fucked up driving.

Nevermind. Pull over to that 7-Eleven over there. Park in the dark part.

CarStop. ArmRed painRub.

GroanPush doorWide. LegLift. Ugh. *DownDrop.* Fuck that hurts. Hand me those paper towels willya? I'm gonna be talkin for a while. You okay?

Yeah.

Gimme your belt.

Wha?

I need to cinch my leg up.

Use your own.

I didn't wear one today.

Too fucken bad.

You don't want me to fall over while I'm talking on the phone do you?

Oh for fuck sakes.

LooseBuckle. BeltToss.

Thanks. *LegCinch.* Ugh.

Fuck man. I think we're had.

No fucken way.

This arm is seized right up. And you look like a fucken zombie.

It's gonna look even more slasherflick when I try to walk. Wish I had a picture. The bloody footprints alone. *Pocket-Search.* You got a quarter?

Huh?

For the phone.

Oh. *PantSearch.* Here.

Thanks.

Wait a minute.

What?

Nomatter who you're headin out to kill. I think you better zip up.

Hah. *DownLook.* Good one. *FlyZip.*

LurchWalk.

PayPhone.

NumberHungry headSearch. MentalScour scroungeDigit. RehearseDial.

CoinJam.

MemoDial.

BuzzBuzz.

The number you have reached is not. *FlickHook.*

MentalSearch rehearseDial.

CoinRetrieve.

CoinJam.

MemoDial.

BuzzBuzz. TwelveBuzz.

Yes?

This is Flame.

It better be. Nobody has this number.

Just as I was told. Sorry to bother you.

I won't say it's no problem.

Special circumstance.

Understood. I heard about Roberto and Papajohn.

What's the deal over there?

They were warned. Nobody can say it was that much of a surprise. But you know how it is. They just didn't believe it would ever happen to them.

Uh huh.

If they'd taken precautions certain things could have been done.

Uh huh.

But enough about things no one in the world can change now. What do we have to discuss this night?

We nearly got bushwhacked.

Small wonder. The locals will be positioning themselves as best they can for a Robertofree world. And they'll only want tried and tested old boys beside them. You guys might as well be Martians as far as they're concerned.

We were thinking about staying out here.

There's your problem right there. No place.

For sure?

It's not your corpus exactly. Although I'm sure there's an element of that too. Pickings are getting lean. No. It's your expertise. Guys like you chill the underpants off these hometown softies. If they thought you wouldn't be slitting their throats before breakfast they might just ignore you and give you a job. Happy ever after. But murder techs like you. Naw.

What's your advice?

Go with your strengths.

Seriously?

Why not? Like I said. These guys are cardboard cutouts compared to you and that weird partner of yours. Stake your territory. Pee around the perimeter. Howl at the moon. Or whatever it is you crazy guys like to do. Work a little of your particular profession in the right places and you should be okay.

Well. That clarifies somewhat.

Glad to help.

We'll need material support.

I can get you a flop. Three days only. Then you relocate where I don't know.

We're pretty banged up.

Medical attention? Sorry. I can get a first aid kit your way. But other than that you're just going to have to bleed.

Anything you could do we'd be glad.

I'll get on it. Anything else?

How about cash.

I'll see what Papajohn left in the miscellaneous kitty. Whatever it is'll be waiting for you at your new temporary address.

Okay. Fair enough.

All right then.

Guess we might as well get started.

ASAP. They're not that stupid. And some of them might eventually learn to shoot straight.

Oh yeah. That reminds me. We'll want to see to a thing.

Oh?

We need an address.

That's stretching it.

We won't be pestering you again.

I can confirm that.

You know our work.

I was satisfied with the service. Yeah. *PhoneSigh*. For that I'll do you this one.

Appreciated.

But forever hence.

No word.

Not a whiff.

Nope.

Not a glimpse.

You got it.

Not so much as a hissing pissbubble in the frothy urinals of hell.

Agreed.

Okay. Who?

They call him Gort.

Gordon Trevor Brownbeck. Prospective new boss. Good choice.

I figger we can start there.

And end there.

Oh no. We got shot up pretty bad.

Nevertheless. You will stand down.

Whattya talking about?

Can you not hear? You can have Gort but you stop there.

You insist?

Uh huh.

HulkSigh. Reason?

Plenty. None of them for you to know.

Huh. None of our business.

That puts it exactly.

No exceptions.

None.

I guess you call it.

I do.

And we're in no position.

You've got it completely.

Huh.

All right then.

So okay. If you'll just do us this one.

Just a second.

PhoneBreathe.

LegThrob.

Okay here it is. 5614 Arboretum Gate. That's somewhere up in Sunshine Hills. Need a repeat?

No.

Got a map?

GPS in the car.

Then you're all set.

Not quite.

Oh?

Gotta get some ammo. We kinda shot ourselves out.

What are you guys carrying?

Nines. And twentyfives.

You'll find plenty of nine rounds and other kinds where you're going. Basement. Workshop. Behind the nuts and bolts.

Thanks.

Arm up quick. A person doesn't want to walk these streets defenseless. Danger everywhere.

Good advice.

You're welcome.

We'll take it from here.

I'm sure you'll have no problem.

I guess that's it.

Confirmed. Happy hunting.

Night; parking lot: BloodSeat

AutoAmmo glareBlast.
HulkSquint autoBurst.
BlinkMonster autoBurst.
SuperBlind.
WildShoot.
CarDoor slamSlam.
MotorGrowl rubberScreech.
Popopopopopopopbangbang.
MetalCrunch grindGear.
Fuck man I can't believe it they're gettin away!
ShootShootShootShootShootShootClickClick.
Fuck Gort. They sideswiped your Lincoln!
You sure? I can't fucken see.

Yeah sorry bout that. I guess it wasn't such a fucken great idea to kill the lights. One bursta this bad Israeli baby and the muzzleflash is like something outta strobelight hell. Never fired the thing at night before.

Well. *HulkSigh.* That sure as shit went off the rails.
You think we got em at all?
Doubt it. They damn near got me. Shot through my collar.
Fuck they spoiled your leather?
That. *HandTouch bodySwipe.* And my car too.
Fuckers.
Yeah well. Trouble is they're more than just fuckers.
Whattya think they're gonna do?
Fucked if I know. Bad shit would be my closest guess.

Maybe they'll just ramjet back to the eastern shithole from where they fucken came.

Wishful fucken thinkin my man. For sure they have to have some kind of resource around here.

That was us wasn't it?

Naw. These kinda guys are only just barely allied to anybody. Spread themselves around. They've gotta have some other lifeline.

Nother outfit?

Somebody they can call.

Yeah maybe yesterday. But today they're all alone. Papajohn can't help em.

Maybe. But you just don't blast away at these cats like we just did tryin to fucken killem. Effen eh they're gonna be comin back at us in some way shape or fucken form.

Who do we know who can help us here?

Lemme think. *RedEye knuckleRub*. Fuck that sucker is bright when you let it off. I mean my 74 here was flashy enough but. *HulkBlink*. What kinda ammo you usin?

I donno. Stuff that came with it. I only ever shot it off when I first got it. At high noon. Out behind my place.

I'm tellinya man I could not see item one when you opened that thing up.

Me neither. Just went stone fucken blind. I thought of just blastin away with my eyes closed but figgered I might get you just as quick as them.

I'm fucken glad you ceased fire. I got off a coupla shots but I just couldn't see what I was doin. Next thing I knew they were in the car.

And fucken pistol shots flyin in our direction too.

I felt one past my fucken face. An my jacket'll never be the same.

These guys seem to be as good as they say they are.

Duh. Ya think?

I reckon.

Well I'll tell ya one fucken thing. Those killmeisters sure

know now what a buncha fucken stumblebums they're up
against. We better get somebody.

Sure as shit somebody around here knows who we can call.

Maybe. Let's go see how Scroaty's doin.

Drunk probly.

Hope so. We gotta get him to a medic.

FarmTrek.

PursuitRagged. Hey you guys!

Whatthefuckyawant Friendly?

Hold up a sec. We got trouble.

Hah! *DuoSnort hulkLaugh.*

What's so funny? What was all the shootin about?

Neverthefuckyoumind what anything is about. We gotta go
see Scroaty right now. What's the problem?

The goddamn ruckmumps are at the gate. They wanna talk
ta somebody in charge.

Aw fer fucksakes. Anytime but now.

What other time but now? *SmirkMonster.* Musta sounded
like world war five in here.

I guess.

It's gotta be you Gort.

Oh what a fucken surprise. It's always gotta be me.

Roberto left you in charge.

That's a fucken laugharama.

A good one yeah. But you're who they woulda been told.

True. Go on up to the can and get Scroaty. Don't let him
drink too much. Get him dressed in street clothes. We gotta
drive somewhere. West Van maybe. Drop him at Emergency.

Sounds like a plan. Good luck with the cops.

I won't be long. Load him into the Navigator.

Gotcha.

GateWard.

JacketShuck. BowlShirt.

ShambleWalk nonHurry.

GateWay.

RedBlue copStrobe flickerShow.
LoneDark stripeLeg.
Evenin.
You are Gorton?
Uh huh.
You are okay?
Fine. How are you?
Ree son able. Cannot complain. No bodee would care if I did.

Hah.
I am Paquette. Constable.
I know.
You do eh?
Somebody pointed you out to me one time.
Is dat right?
Said you were a good guy.
Well dat was nice of dem. Care to say oo it was?
Can't remember.
Well anyway. Sorry to bodder you tonight.
I appreciate your not coming onto the property.
Rules is rules. No warrant.
So what do we owe this visit to?
Your neighbours eard zome noize a while ago. Soun ded like shooding.

Oh?
Know anyding aboud it?
A coupla the guys might have been target practicing. We told em not to do it at night.

Well some peoble eard a lod of darget shooding going on.

Yeah well. Soma the guys got pretty fancy firearms. All licensed. We got an approved shooting range. I don't know if you know that.

I kind of eard aboud id once or dwice. Was dad where dey were shooding?

Can't really say. I been inside mosta the night.

Is dere anyone around dad can?
I suppose so but by now everybody's gettin pretty drunk.
Drunk.
Yeah.
Dey're gedding drunk now?
Uh huh.
Ow aboud a half our ago?
What do you mean?
Were dey drunk when dey were darget bracticing?
Well. Maybe some of em were.
Dat's nod good bractice.
I know.
Even for an abbroved range wid registered weabons.
We tell em not to. But. You know guys.
Dat's da bizness I'm in all right.
Well then I guess I don't have to tell ya.
No you doen bud I do wan to know why you're allowing semilegal darget bractice on your abbroved range outside da legal ours of oberation by abbarently inebriaded legal firearm owners. Disdurbing da beace order and good gover ment of dis odderwise guiet rural sedding here. So whad's going on rilly?
Nothin more than we discussed earlier Constable.
Nodding more.
Nope.
PoliceArm frownFold.
HulkFrown sneerCurl.
You know id'll gum a dime sooner dan lader you guys are going do go doo far. Give us a reason to gum inside and dake a good look.
There's waysa doin that through proper channels Constable.
Yeah sure.
There is.
Nevermind. Am I going do ave do gum back here lader tonight an dell you guys again to geep dis blace guiet?

Absolutely not.

Good do ear. Bess nod do adrack doo much addention.

That's our policy.

Well stick do it bedder okay? It's ard maging up exguses do da surrounding bobulation.

Sorry.

Okay. *PocketWarble*. Jus a sec I bedder ged dis. *PhoneJab*. Yeah. Uh huh. Yeah. Righd. Righd. Yezzir. *PhoneJab*. Your lazz name is Brownbeck righd?

Uh huh.

Doen go ome.

Huh?

Juzz god da word. You ave a frien zomeplaze. Doen go ome.

For my health I guess.

Dat was my imbression.

Message received.

Good.

Thanks for coming.

All part of gommunidy zervice.

Good to know.

Go dell dose bardy animals do doen id down.

Sure will.

NodGlare.

NodGlare.

SwivelTurn cruiserAmble.

HulkWatch.

RoarMotor. LightFlick.

EmergoFlash offSwitch.

CruiseAway.

DarkShamble. ChillShiver. SylvanStill earRoar.

CarLot reLit.

LincolnWound. Fuck! *RentPart handRun*.

RaggedStep. How bad is it Gort?

Fuck me Friendly. On this thing it'll probly be like five grand or so. Just got it too.

Yeah that's too bad.

StraightStand. Where's Geekster and Scroat? We gotta get outta here.

They were startin to come over here. Last I saw.

Good.

Whattya want me to do with the stiffs in the hooker house? Huh?

That poor girl you guys shot up she's absolutely fulla holes. And you got another one on the other side of the wall too. You dumbheads. You don't go shooting big guns in a paperbox like that. Can't believe anybody got out alive.

Whattdo I want you to do with em?

Yeah.

What you always do with em.

Well I'm getting pretty tireda all that.

Oh fuck.

I'm gettin tireda cleanin up other people's sins Gort. Specially yours. It's just not too damn fair.

Look I'm not goin through this with you anymore.

Well yer gonna hafta.

No I don't hafta.

This sorta crazy stuff can't keep goin on.

Fucken relax willya? It's gonna calm down.

It better.

Never you mind. If you got a mind.

Yer insults just bead up and roll off the backa my head Gort. Like a duck.

Why are we having this conversation?

Cause you need me Gort.

You need me more Friendly. You need me not to use this steel on you right now.

I know I know. You got the hammer and the gun. But you gotta sleep sometime.

Don't worry. I sleep fine.

Just tell me things are gonna calm down.

Things are gonna calm down.

Well. Maybe yer right. With them murdermen off the property things might quiet down.

That's lookin on the bright side.

But these girls you know. They're startinta talk. You guys can't disappear too many more hookers or they'll just downright refuse to come out here.

Look Friendly I'm too busy to keep talking in circles about this right now. Just stay on top of it the best you can. Okay?

Okay Gort. *MockRagged snapSalute heelClick*. Whatever you say Gort.

HeftMonster grogHulk. Gimme a hand you guys.

Muhhhhh. *RearSeat groanHulk*. Bwwahh!

When did he start mumblin?

Around about the fifth double rye. He fucken chugged the fuckers. Shoulder must hurt like a sonofabitch.

A guy who's been shot shouldn't be drinkin.

You gonna be the one to stop him?

He's bleedin too.

Guys with bullet wounds often do Gort.

Not on my fucken upholstery. Friendly. Go up to your shack and get us a plastic sheet or somethin.

Righto Gorty ol pal! *JauntRagged skipAway*.

HulkHead shakeSigh. Fucken guy's losin it eh?

Can't say for sure. Donno if he was crazy to begin with or just goin that way all along. Whatthefuckever. Too busy to find out and don't give a fucken shit anyway. Got any ideas where we take Scroaty?

I think your suggestion was good. Place like West Van. He's dressed reasonable. We strip his wallet and ID. Drop him at the curb out of camera range. It's a non ruckmump jurisdiction so when the bullet wound gets em all excited and the municicops investigate they won't want to share the glory so they'll go it alone. Scroaty keeps his trap shut of course. No other cop department will help. Especially our ruckmumps. Trail'll go cold awful fucken fast. Then he just walks out of the place when he can and it's over. Simple.

Wherethefuck is Friendly? We gotta get goin.

He's so fucked in the head tonight I donno if he's comin back.

Aw fuck just put my leather under him. Shot to shit anyways.

Night; Lion's Gate Bridge: ClubHop

UteDrive parkGlide.

Glad that's over.

What? *HulkSniff.* Nothin's over. We still gotta kill those guys.

Naw naw. Scroaty. Glad he's in the hospital and all that.

Aw he'll be okay. Tough to kill that fucken treetrunk. We got bigger fish to fricasee right now. This is one effed up sichiation.

Well I donno. We run em off pretty good. Not likely they'll be comin back right away. They're not gettin paid to whack us. I'll bet they work strictly for cash. Once the smoke clears. Think it through. Might think of comin after us but nobody's payin.

That's just it. There's no money comin from anywhere anymore. East is fucked for now and likely forever. If they wanna earn they gotta set somethin up for themselves.

So.

So they see what we got goin here and maybe they think they can take us. After this abortionate halfassed attempted assassination performance tonight they know damn sure they can take us.

Oh fuck I donno. Too much thinkin for me. I figger the night is done for em anyway. Likely they're goin someplace lookin for somebody good with a bandage. I'm sure I got that Flame sucker. If not with a bullet at least with glass from the window.

Oh we hit em good enough to skin their knuckles and break their ribs but they're still in business. You bet on that.

What makes you so sure?

The ruckmump told me.

Yeah?

In the middle of our little discussion. By the gate. Got a call all secretive. More or less confirmed it.

Fucken eh.

Got that fucken right.

Well I still say we take it easy tonight. Lay low.

Goes without fucken sayin.

Only thing is. Where?

It's what? One thirty?

Yeah.

Your girls still dancin?

Until three at least. For the public. Later for us. You wanna stop in?

Why not? You got anybody new?

Uh not sure. Since the last time you were there.

Got anybody who'd pass for an ol lady?

Well fuck I donno. You lookin?

Always.

What. Bitch trouble?

Always.

Hah.

Well maybe I'm just horny. Put it this way. You got any tight bitches dancing in those clubsa yours?

Tight? I only hire tight.

I can imagine how you find out.

Imagine away.

Lucky fucker.

Hey you donno the whole shitfilled story. There's more to managing clubs than interviewing prospective dancers.

Yeah yeah. Interview. That's a good one. Let's go get a fucken drink at least.

Drive on.

Which one? The Francis or The Water?

The Water's just got skanks these days. Low end trade.

The Francis then.

You know the way.

I do.

Anyway. I guess since you're in charge now it's a good idea you should come and look over the properties.

I guess you're right. How they doin?

Well like I said The Water is my dunghole. But it makes out good with the shitcan set. Cheap beer. Twenty dollar blow jobs. Stays crowded cause none of the rummies scare off anya the other rummies. I was losin the college trade outta The Francis when I had it all mixed up. We take out an average ten large per week.

Not too fucken bad for low end.

Like I said. Mixing the two didn't work. Since I upgraded The Francis and chucked out all the shitrats we been grabbin twenty a week outta there.

My man. Good goin.

We'll see how it works for a while. These clubs are fuckers for headaches I don't mind sayin. If it's not one fucken thing it's another. Girls get pissed off and quit. Or get stoned and don't show up. Or get busted and can't work. Or get sick and hell knows what you do with em. Then you got the competition. One club is hot for a month and goes dead. Another perks up all of a sudden outta the blue and you got an overnight personnel shortage ya gotta deal with. And the staff are constantly tryin to rob ya stupid. And through it all you got local community on one side and clientele on the other givin ya simultaneous shit from opposite directions. Like I said. A constant headache. If I'da known what a hassle the whole fucken thing was I'da never got into it.

Well obviously Roberto thought you could do a good job.

Oh that guy. I thought we didn't talk about him no more.

Right you are. In all the excitement I forgot.

Forgot about what?

Oh nothin.

Hah hah.

Which reminds me. I gotta make a call as soon as we get sat down. See how things are goin in a certain Kaybeck jailhouse.

TownDrive.

StripClub carPark.

RearDoor.

You got a special knock?

Naw I got keys. *DoorPull.*

StripTune enviroThrob.

Sounds like a show on. I'll get us a table.

HallWay curtainDoor archPassage.

ClubFloor.

HalfFull tableTrade. EyeWide stageFix.

She's not bad.

Take a seat my friend. She's onea the amateurs. There's more and better to come. Whattya wanna drink?

Heineken.

ScanMonster floorStaff. Hey Na!

AsiaFemme faceTurn.

Who's that?

That's Na. My new greeter gal. Sweet bitch but she don't wanna dance.

I can see why you keep her around.

Hey Na. Meet Gort. An important frienda mine.

HandProffer. Hello Mister Gort.

Actually it's Gordon.

I thought there might be a nicer name to match that handsome face.

Heh heh.

As you now know Na does a helluva job greasin the customers around here. As well as keepin the books and overseein the place. But I'd rather she just got up and danced. Why won't you dance baby?

I believe we've been through that a few times Mister Greco.

Oh come on sweetheart I told you to call me Dave.

Well Mister Dave Greco I informed you when first interviewing for the job that I didn't mind the hours or the environment or the clientele or the staff. But I only do hostess work and admin and accounting and that's it. Dancing is for professionals.

But you got such a nice booty.

I accept the compliment.

God what a toughie. You'd be a nightmare to have for an ol lady.

Perhaps that's why I am not anyone's. Ol lady. As you put it.

Aw you donno what you're missin.

Don't presume Mister Greco. Do I not look like I've been around at least a little bit?

Yeah maybe. *LeerMonster.* Could you get us a couplea Heineken?

I certainly could. Nice to meet you Mister Gordon.

Just Gordon.

Nice to meet you just Gordon.

Well come on back and sit down when you have a chance.

I might do that.

FemmeWalk hulkEye leerWatch.

Effen nice man.

Doesn't she just do ya?

I'll fucken say.

This next dancer I highly recommend. Another Chinagirl. You like em eh?

Like em? I fucken love em.

No kiddin.

Hands down the world's best pussy. China Japan Korea Vietnam. Sweet. Tight. Delicious. Especially Thailand. You agree?

I donno.

Well I've made a major fucken research project out of it.

A hole's a hole. What's the difference?

Well Gort my man it's like this. I donno about you. But I got an average size dick.

Too much info.

Not small exactly. But not no ponderous killer dong or anything like that. You?

Nevermind.

Okay okay. But seriously.

Yeah seriously. What?

White girls these days are so bigscale. Tall. Wide. All those steroids in the food. Need a footlong dick just to make an impression. But you take your average miniature Asian snatch.

Never had the experience.

Well my man you've come to the right place. You slide your average size dick into this tiny cooze. Make you feel like the biggest dongswingin stud this side of the porn industry. I can fix up a little experience for ya right tonight.

Naw.

Sure?

Yeah. Fuck man. Tell you the fucken honest truth I'm dead tired right now. All this shootin and drivin and dodgin bullets. I'd rather just sit around and have a beer and maybe a polite conversation or something. When Na gets back.

Aha. Found your weakness after all.

Whattya mean? I gotta do some thinkin and she seems like a broad who lets a guy do it and'll maybe lend a hand.

She is that. Funny she's been workin here three months and never once went home with a customer. I tried a couplea times and you can see how she handles me. I'd fire the cunt for insubordination but she does a fucken fine job on the books. And look at this place. Clean. Classy. It's all her.

She's a prime piece all right.

Well watch yourself with er. Nobody actually knows where she's been or where she's goin.

Lemme worry about that. Meanwhile. Before I forget. *Close-*

Lean. Who of those drunkard rangatangs we got standin around the fire every night might be good to send on a private mission?

What kinda private mission?

I need somebody to camp outside my house for a day or two.

What's goin on?

I can't go home for a while. Put it that way.

No fucken kiddin.

To be expected.

I guess.

So who do we send?

Well let's see. I got a couplea guys help out around here. Gypsy and Sweat.

Well no. Somebody you might not need. Who else?

There's the harbour unions crew. Randy. Ray. Dirtybird.

Somebody who doesn't live in Surrey and doesn't know me that well.

Hmmm. Where in Surrey?

Sunshine Hills.

Where the fuck and what the fuck are Sunshine Hills?

Just another fucken hideout. Streetlights. Big fucken wide houses. Pussies in gilt cages. We only been there eight months and already my kid is official school bully. Already my old lady's outsexed all these other scared snob neighbour bitches.

What a fucken joke.

You should fucken see it man. Fucken lawnpride. Gotta see that grass grow. Gotta watch green mature do its work.

So what's the fucken attraction?

I donno. It's fucked up enough with grow ops and spoilt B&E kids that nobody says nothin about my comin home at three in the morning in a loud sports car. We sleep past noon nobody bothers us. We send the kid out wadded with cash and tell him not to come back til nightfall. Visitors all times of day or night.

It's nobody's business. Vehicles. Thugs coming and going of all shapes and weights. Cops cruising past the house. But when everything's locked up and done with I can still relax.

Hmmm. Not a bad soundin hideout.

It was til now anyway.

So we gotta get a guy who can hang around.

And not get himself high centered or otherwise made. And can keep awake. And can keep himself alive.

Maybe Dirtybird.

He the one with that butterfly tatty down his neck?

Yeah.

Can he dress up like a burbjohn? No leather.

I seen him in a suit one time he was goin ta court. Looked like a fucken stockbroker.

What was the beef?

Some kinda bar assault.

Well I don't need a stockbroker but I need a guy who can drive around the neighbourhood and not look like he's casin the joint for a grow rip.

I'll fix him up. Whattya lookin for?

Cars. Activity. I need to know when the coast is clear.

Fine. You want it right now?

Naw. I kinda know it's not safe right now. No sense anytime before morning.

I'll make the call.

Do that.

PhoneFlip. EarFinger shoutTalk.

Here you go boys. *DuoDrop frostBottle.*

Thanks. Na is it?

Yes.

These twisttops?

I'm sure you can handle it.

Kaspoit! Always.

Why the serious face? Don't like the show?

You're the best view. *CupShout thumpThrob overCall.* In the place.

Oh ho. A silver tongue.

Huh. Don't think I ever heard myself described like that. I'm surprised.

From what I heard that don't happen too often.

I don't know what Mr. Greco has told you. I've shared with him next to nothing.

Good girl. Can we go someplace quieter and sit down?

I'm working.

I know.

Is it okay with my boss here?

He's busy. I'm in charge right now.

I see. *FemmeLead rearBar.* Feels funny to be consorting with the brass.

You'll get used to it.

I not sure about that. We can sit here.

Great. At least I can hear myself talk.

If that's what you want to do.

So they call you Na.

That is my name yes.

What does it mean?

Nothing significant. I once had a relative say it referred to an ethnic subset from the eastern part of India.

But you're Chinese. Right?

My family is from Thailand.

No kiddin.

No kidding.

Na eh?

Yes. Na.

How do you spell it?

N. A.

That simple eh? Nothing complicated about it.

No. Should there be?

I donno. You're from another country. For all I know it's a different language or something like that.

My family emigrated when I was three. I grew up in Saskatoon. I'm Canadian as stubby beer bottles.

No kiddin?

What did you expect?

Well hey. What do I know? I'm just a dumbass whiteguy.

From what I've heard I wouldn't describe you that way.

Well thanks. I think.

You're welcome.

So your name sounds like somebody lazy saying no. You got other names?

Thai ones.

Like what?

Iandua.

E and do what?

I never use it. Too hard to pronounce.

What's it mean?

It kind of translates into jewel.

Diamond?

Something like that.

You suit it.

I try.

It fits. Seriously.

Thank you.

Got a life outsidea here?

You might say.

What might I say?

I study part time. Work for Mr. Greco here. Save money. Support my mom in Saskatchewan.

That's a life?

I think so.

Whattya study?

Psychology and English.

Whereabouts?

Simon Fraser.

SFU? Good ol Snafu U.

I've heard some people call it that.

I tried goin there once.

Really?

Decades ago. Wastea time.

But you did try.

Not hard.

But you did finish highschool.

Umm nearly.

You must have done something right to get accepted.

Oh I got in on some kinda bullshit juvie scholarship. From bein in lockup when I was a teenager.

I see. So they gave you a big chance.

That was what they kept tellin me.

But you apparently didn't believe it.

It was all bullshit.

Education is important.

Hey I'm a bigtime successful businessman.

Sitting in a stripbar at two A.M. on a Thursday morning.

What's wrong with that?

Why aren't you relaxing in a McMansion with your wife and two point three children?

I got no wife and children.

Well you could at least be in your home theatre watching pay-per-view porn or something.

I got no home.

I don't know what you mean.

I'm out on the street.

That's silly.

Just for tonight.

Really. This is beginning to sound like a cheap hustle.

Aw come on.

No no. It's okay. It's just that until now it was sounding like an expensive hustle. But it's always been a hustle. Right?

We're just talkin.
Of course we are.
Hey you're a lippy little bitch.
I'm sure you're acquainted with the type.
I'm just tryinta be nice.
And looking for a place to lay your head for a night.
If I can.
You've heard of hotels?
I can get a room. Sure.
StepMonster phoneSnap. All done Gort.
Good.
You guys getting acquainted?
We're nearly fucken married. Just had our first fight.

EARLY MORNING; BEDROOM: CORPSE-CUT

Ragged Bed.
Just relax Freddy.
Huh?
Do you have some kind of medical condition?
I dunno. I.
Never saw a doctor in your life. I kind of get it now. Do you have this trouble when the professional girls work on you?
Naw.
I wonder what that's about.
I dunno.
Well it's okay sweetie. You just lie back and relax.
I rilly like you Maisie. I like touchin ya.
I know you do. And you know I like you Freddy.
I sure do.
So we've got something here.
I sure like seein ya naked.
You're so sweet.
It's a heckuva nice change.
Oh ho. What do you mean by that?
By what?
Change. I'm a nice change. Do you see other women naked?
Well. Yeah. Well no. But.
But what?
Oh. I guess I should keep my mouth shut. I guess I talk too much.
Not really.
Yeah I do. Gort always says so.
Who is this Gort person you keep talking about?

He's kinda the boss around here. Sure thinks he is anyways.

I take it he's a member of this. What did you call it? Business association.

Uh huh.

And he tells you what to do.

Sure does.

And criticizes you for speaking your mind.

And just about everthin else.

Well he doesn't sound like a very nice person to me.

Nice ain't got much to do with anybody round here.

I've been getting that sense. You seem. Traumatized.

What does that word mean again?

In your case I guess hurt by a bad experience. Psychologically scarred.

Huh. I guess I might be.

What exactly do they get you to do around here?

Like I said. Farming. Stuff.

Well straight farming doesn't usually traumatize people. Unless you're not cut out for it. But that wouldn't be you would it Frederick?

Naw. I can do the regular stuff okay.

Regular stuff.

Yeah. Gardening and feeding the animals.

Do you ever have to slaughter the animals?

Huh?

You heard me sweetie. You don't have to talk about it if you don't want to.

I kinda don't wanna talk about it.

That's okay.

I'd sure be grateful.

Grateful for what?

Grateful if we didn't hafta talk about it.

Well you get your wish. *ZipLip.* There.

Yer sure nice Maisie.

Well you're nice too.

I'm differnt. From the nasty guys around here anyway.

I've always known that Freddy. *BodySnug tangleTwine.*
Maybe we can try this again.

Yer too nice.

What's that?

I like ya too much Maisie. And the way I feel with ya. Yer a
blessed person.

Blessed?

Holy and sanctified. Like in The Bible. You must be. Yer an
angel Maisie.

Oh I wouldn't go that far.

You must be. Yer so nice.

Well thank you dear. I don't think any man has ever given
me such sweetness.

Well it's not hard for me. I think yer the sweetest.

Tee hee.

So I can't do that to ya.

That. You can't do. That. To me.

Yer just too fine.

Well. How sad. When you can't do. That. To a person you
like.

I never felt it before. Feels kinda funny.

Funny. I'll tell you what's funny. You are funny.

I am?

You bet.

Funny hah hah or funny strange?

I have to be honest. Both ways.

Well I guess that's better'n weird and no good at all.

I'm glad you see it that way dear. It's nothing to be
ashamed of. And I'm sure that with a little time your little.
Blockage. Will correct itself.

It will?

I'm sure of it. I mean. From what I have in my hand. Even
in it's shrunken state. It feels like this thing could be a fear-

some apparatus once the man attached to it loses his hangups.

Apparatus huh.

Yup.

You're so funny Maisie.

Glad you think so.

Huh.

So.

Yup.

What should we do now?

Well. It's kinda late. I gotta lotta work to do t'morrow.

Should we just go to sleep?

I figger.

Do you mind having me here. With you. In bed?

Aw gee it's awful sweet Maisie. You all naked and everything. If you wanna stay.

Of course I'll stay. We can just cuddle.

That's sure fine with me.

Let me take out my contacts though.

You got contacts?

I'm nearly blind without them. I'll just slip into the bathroom. *FloorStep terryWrap.* Do you mind if I use your bathrobe?

Go right ahead.

BathLight floorBeam. RaggedSmile.

Whew. Thank goodness that didn't take long. It's a little chilly. I hope you've got it nice and warm in bed.

See fer yerself.

WrapFling bedJump. Oh you're such a hottie.

Hah.

Both ways of course. But temperature wise especially. You must have a fast metabolism or something. Either that or I have a better effect on you than we first thought.

I think it's you.

You're such a gentleman. How's that little appendage of yours doing? Huh. Still no action.

I'm pretty sure I can't do nothin for ya Maisie. At least not tonight.

Oh well. A girl can always hope.

Let's just go ta sleep.

It's so quiet out here. I hope I can.

Oh you might hear some yellin and whoopin it up. Out by the fire. Shouldn't be too bad. Usually stops by two or so.

Well I'm yawning. Let's just fade away and see how it goes. I'm looking forward to breakfast.

Oh I might have to take you out for that. There's a Denny's down the road. Not much goin on round here til noon or so.

Whatever dear. Just go to sleep.

It sure is nice havin you here Maisie.

Oh my yes. Yes. I'm sleepy.

I am too.

Mmmmmmm.

DozeBreathe.

Mmmmmmm.

RaggedWide eyeOpen throbHard.
PassHour.
HardAwake.
CloseEye sleepWill.
SheepCount. HardAwake. SleepWill. StareAwake.
BedSlink.
LightStep bathBound. SoftClose. LightFlick. EyeSquint.
HardMember hangSink.
WaterSoap rousePull instaBlast.
PullBlast pullBlast.
SighHeavy. ForeHead mirrorRest.
EasyBreathe. HeadLean nightCalm handHold dickDrip. Easy-Breathe.
FaceWash.
LightFlick.
DeepBreathe.

DoorDraw.
RoomFill sleepBreath.
TipToe. SleepBreath. CoverAll. RubberSole clogStep. Sleep-
Breath. SneakStep.
DarkMorn. StillField airFresh.
WorkShop pathStep. DewCover.
CorruSteel squeakDoor.
BunkerHeavy cementScent.
PauseBreath.
LightFlick.
StutterCatch fluoresceFlicker humBurn.
DankFloor drainGrate hookHang labourSite.
JumboFridge humCool.
CoolerDoor openPull downKnee.
TwoHand bodyHeft. FemmeCorpse.
FloorDrag.
TwoAnkle twineWind.
OverDrain hangBody.
FridgePull.
TwoHand bodyHeft. BoardStiff femmeCorpse.
FloorDrag.
TwoAnkle twineWind.
OverDrain hangBody.
WorkBench.
RubberApron.
RubberBoot.
RubberHat.
BladeSelect.
FluoresceGleam. GrindStone. GlitterBlade.
FlexHand knifeSupple.
RaggedSigh.
HatchetChoose. EmeryHone. GleamHead.
DoubleHand toolWield.
SighRagged.
StoopAside hangBody.

UpperSpine axeAim. DrawBack. NeckStrike.
BoneCrack.
AxeDrop.
KnifeHack.
ThreeStroke neckSever.
HeadDrop. GripCoif wristSwing.
StepToss headBucket.
HardHack offArm limbWork.
OffArm.
NextUp offHead.
OffArm.
OffArm.
WorkBench limbStack.
CorruSteel squeakDoor.
Oh here you are!
StartleClutch knifeDrop.
At least I think it's you. *SquintFemme armStretch airProbe.*
That is you Freddy. Isn't it? I woke up and you weren't there.
Are you doing some work?

Maisie you can't come in here!

Don't be silly. I saw the lights on. But I guess I should have
got my glasses.

Go back to bed. I'm comin right now.

If you couldn't sleep I can understand you wanting to get
some work done. Let me watch. *FemmeStep.*

No!

Ooh smells like a butcher shop. I guess that's the reality of
carnivorism. Don't worry about me. *SquintStep probeArm.* I
can take it.

PanicLunge. No Maisie get out of here! *BloodSlip.*

Watch out Freddy. You don't want a workplace injury. Oh. Is
this a bunch of pig parts? They say pigs are as close to human
in as many ways as you can get without being.

Maisie!

Cannibal. *ProbeTouch.* Are these fingers?

TerryRobe rubberApron bloodSmear.
Oh!
Maisie.
Oh. Oh. *HandFlick spitFlick.* Get it off! Get it off!
Maisie Maisie Maisie.
Ahhhhhggggg!
Maisie please be quiet. Please be quiet. We don't want any-body knowin yer here.
Eiiii. Eiiii. Ahhhhhggggg!
Calm down now. Calm down.
Let me go! Let me go!
I can't letcha go until ya tell me yer not gonna scream no more.
Oh my god!
I wanted ta get em in the ground before ya seen em.
Oh my god. Oh my god.
You shouldn'ta come in here Maisie.
Oh my god. Let me go. Let me go.
I can't yet. Are ya gonna calm down?
Let me get out of here. I just want to get out of here.
Okay okay we'll getcha outta here. Lemme take this apron off.
Oh my god. I can't breathe. Oh my god.
I'm gonna ease off on ya here Maisie. There ya go.
I'm going to be sick. I'm goin to. *LurchGut.*
It's okay Maisie just let it go. Here.
DoubleOver spewFlow. Ahhhhhggggg!
Let it go Maisie. Let it go.
CoughSpew. LimpWilt.
Maisie?
SwoonBlank. EyeRoll.
Huh. *QuickShuck bloodApron.*
ShuckBoot shuckHat.
GripFemme.
LiftCarry.

Finger Pull squeak Door.
Flick Light.
Stumble Carry.

Morning; Georgia Hotel: Porn-Count

Oh Na baby. You fuck like somethin offa the porn channel.
Thank you I think.
Even if it hadta be rubberized.
That's compulsory.
What's that thing you do inside just as I'm about to come?
The West Indians call it *soupape*.
Soup what?
It's a tightening technique. Takes practice. And good muscles.
You actually do crotch exercise?
Why not? You pump iron don't you?
Well soup whatever it is it's superfucken hot.
That's why I charge.
Huh. You're serious about that.
Aren't you serious about what you do for money?
I guess.
I went down to the Caribbean and spent a lot of risky time
with some sketchy personalities to pick up that skill.
You get around a lot eh?
More than you and your friends.
What's that sposedta mean?
I don't sense much worldliness among the gentleman's
club.
Huh. We been around enough.
The wrong places I would suspect.
You don't think mucha Geek and me and the other guys
do ya?
Oh don't pout. I actually think more of you boys than you'd
think. You're roughedged for sure. But it has to do with your

business prowess. Awesome. From what I've seen you've stolen the machine that prints money.

Smart girl.

I mean this suite. A place like this they hardly ever see cash. How much was it?

Six bills.

And you just haul a wad out of your jeans and deal it out. Don't you fellows know about credit cards?

We know all about em. Onea the guys runs a chip reading scam.

Hah hah.

Laugh all you want. We rip ten grand a week out of it. Last I heard.

Ten thousand dollars? A week? Maybe I'm not charging enough.

Hey. Seriously. I'm not payin a G per fuck.

Yes you are.

No I'm fucken not.

Didn't you say I worked your dick off just now? Didn't I explain the physical process to you and the specialized skill and preparation involved?

Aw c'mon that was all bullshit.

Suit yourself.

Maybe I'll just dink ya anyways.

Try it.

Okay I will.

GrappleProng.

MountWield. LegSpread.

You sure cooperate for somebody who thinks they're bein raped.

Go ahead. Stick it in. You don't have to murder me for it.

RamUrge Ah. Ah. *RamUrge.* Ah.

Have a ball.

Ah ah. *LongStroke.* Aw fuck. *LongStroke.* You can do the loose thing too.

You asked for it.

Feels like you had five kids.

Flail away King Dick.

LoosePull. Might as well stick it out in the rain.

I love you too Gort.

You are one lippy fucken headstrong cunt.

I sense you becoming enlightened.

Whatever the fuck that means.

It might be the only way you idiot monsters learn anything.

WarbleTone.

Lemme think on that you fucken bitch.

WarbleTone.

My phone's ringin.

At three in the morning?

Shut up. *ThumbStab*. Yo.

Dis is Sa Jerome.

Yeah.

Iz done.

For sure?

Zure as is pozzible do know a guy iz det.

Good.

PhoneJab.

Sounds like business.

It's always business.

Oh good. You have learned.

Listen. Could you put away your smart mouth for five minutes and gimme some fucken mental assistance here? I gotta think.

I'll give you the same deal as the sex. First one free.

All right then. Geek says you know about books.

Some. The basics they give you in admin school. I focused on marketing.

Sounds good enough. Could you look at some figures and tell me what the situation was with a group of small and large businesses? Like a diversified multi-purpose scattered all over the fucken place pile of different money making deals legitimate and otherwise? I need a head like that on my side ta figger out some stuff.

Like Mr. Greco's stripper empire.

Right. And that chip readin thing and lotsa other stuff.

I could try. Does someone have to stand over me with a gun?

What do you mean?

Well I surmise there is change in the wind. No one seems to be speaking anymore about this Roberto person I've never met.

Nevermind him.

I won't. There are already enough players to keep track of. But what I would worry over is whether or not I am with the new true power.

You'll just haveta see.

I have already seen quite a lot. Instincts would dictate I put my clothes on and leave.

You'd be turnin down a heapin shitloada money.

Really?

Again. You'll just haveta see.

Aha. So. If you now have access to the heart and mind of the business. Which I was vaguely aware was run and overseen by this fellow with the Latinate name.

I said forget him.

So I can safely surmise he is no longer Mister Big? You are? Maybe? If you can figure out how to run things in time to herd all these cats you call business associates into a cohesive unit that doesn't start gnawing on itself.

I donno what the fuck yer tryin to figger here but I need an answer to my bookkeeping question and I need it fucken now.

Then I ask again. Do we need protection?

Huh?

Is anybody going to do to you and or whoever is standing close to you what you just I suppose did to Mister Roberto what's-his-name?

Not if I can help it.
Are you carrying a firearm?
No. But I can get one.
Do. Then I suppose we better get started.
Doing what?
Let's go get some breakfast.
Now?
It's already past four. There's no way I'll be able to sleep.
And I need you to talk to me about what you want me to look
for. Et cetera. Besides. I need food.
Okay.
There's a Denny's down the street.
Yer an easy girl to please. That way anyway.
ClothesRuffle.
FemmeRise flounceMove.
How bout a little bendover?
Fine. One thousand. Cash. In advance.
RuffleSearch. WalletWield.

FencePound.
HulkStab securiCom buttonPad. Lemme in.
Fuck off. *ElectroVoice.* Gort.
Who the fuck is talkin?
StaticCrackle. Nevermind.
Aw fer fucksakes. *TurnSeat fingerPoint.* Open that glovebox
willya.
StabDrop.
There's a buncha cards in there.
You're not kidding. *TwoHand paperShuffle.* Which one?
Give em here.
ShuffleWhip.
CardSwipe. Fuck.
CardSwipe. Fuck.
CardSwipe. Fuck.
SwipePass. Fuck.

SwipePass.
FenceRattle openSlide.
LincolnPark.

Is there going to be shooting? Because my rates go way high if there is.

Don't worry your pretty little snatch over it. These guys are fucked without Roberto.

Why don't I derive intrinsic confidence from your assessment?

I got us in didn't I?

That's a good thing?

Come on.

DuoWalk.
StillCompound.
FistPush swingDoor.
DarkBar loungeGloom.
BarMonster shotGun chestAim. What the fuckya think yer doin Gort?

Comin in. That's what.

Roberto said nobody in til he gets back.

Roberto ain't comin back.

Says fucken you.

Look ah. What's yer name? Darren?

Darryl.

Look Darryl. You can stay on here fuckin the dog like you been doin for years and nobody's gonna bother ya. Or you can keep aimin that rod at me and get yer testes carved out and roasted on a wood grill before your very fucken eyes. What'll it be dickweed? I mean Darryl.

Whatcha doin here so early in the fucken mornin?

It's nearly nine A.M. in Kaybeck. Where they're cleanin Roberto's guts off some jailhouse showerroom floor.

Yer shittin.

I got a number you can call.

Well fuck me. *DownBarrel.* What the fuck is goin on?

Right now what's goin on is I got my accountant here and quit lookin at er and don't have any fantasies about fuckin er. Yer job right now is to open up the back office and unlock the file cabinets and then cook up the biggest fucken potta coffee you can make. Okay?

You the new fucken boss I magine.

You magine right.

Fuck.

Change Darryl. It's good for ya.

I'll be the fucken judgea that.

You gonna get the keys?

Yeah yeah. *DrawerPull.*

When you finish with the coffee I wantcha back on shotgun duty. Nobody gets in.

You got in.

That's my fucken point. Who else has passcards?

Fucked if I know.

Then go out and disable that fucken cardswipe scanner. Spraypaint some glue into it or somethin.

Glue?

Sumpm nobody can get off right now but we can solvent away when we're good an ready.

Okay I gotcha.

Good man Darryl.

Nice place you boys have here.

Nevermind that. Get in there and have a look at those books.

DoorPush. FileKey lockTwist.

Looks like we'll be here for a long time.

As long as it takes for you to give me a good idea where we're at here.

Can I set up at the desk?

Sure.

WarbleTone. I gotta get this. Darryl. *WarbleTone fingerPoint.* Get to it.

Yeah boss.

ThumbStab. Yeah.

Geek here. What's the sichiation?

Nothin. Dick all. What's the word from Dirtybird?

Also dick all. He's down the street from your place. Says there's no cars around. No lights on. No signa anythin.

Okay. Tell him to stick around until I call ya.

Okay. Any idea how long?

At least for mosta today. Maybe tomorrow too. Did he pack a lunch?

If not I'll get somethin out to him. He has to shift around a bit. Drive off and repark in different places. Maybe hang out at the 7-Eleven down the street. Your neighbourhood's too quiet. The local dogwalkers already made him.

Tell him not to worry about that. They're a buncha fucken nominds. Tellim just make fucken sure ta keep an eye on the house.

Okay.

Anythin else?

Well this is a funny thing. Friendly's apparently goin around the farm tryin to score some crack.

What?

Says he's got a girlfriend over and she's itchin for a hit.

Unfuckingbelievable.

No kiddin.

Who is this broad?

Fucked if anybody knows.

Well whoever she is tell Friendly she's gotta be off the property yesterday or we'll get rid of er for im.

I already toldim.

He give the usual guff?

The usual.

I'm startin ta think we outta do somethin about that mental midget.

My thoughts exackly.

But we gotta get things under control around here first. Roberto's officially out of the photo.

For sure?

What they tell me.

You heard?

Called me three this mornin.

Okay then.

So put the word around. Business as usual but carry a piece. Tell everybody. Pack at all times. Shoot to fucken kill if those two wackos show up again.

Okay. Where to from here?

I'll let you know.

Any ideas?

I'm at the clubhouse right now with my new business consultant.

You fucken ahole you. I saw you leavin with er. Lucky sonofabitch.

Lucky? Maybe.

Whattya mean? You did you fucker didn'tcha?

Much as I could afford. You gotta strap a goddamn ATM on yer back to service this bitch.

Is she there?

Suckin my dick right now.

Teller she's gonna get a fucken STD.

Yeah I'll teller. Fuck you too.

Hah hah. At least somebody finally got er.

Well I donno about that. I don't think anybody actually gets this bitch. I think she gets everybody else.

Huh. Well anyway. I guess she's not comin in to work at my joint tonight eh.

You can wipe er off the books. I'll be needin er specialized services from now on.

Fucker.

Yeah I intend to.

Noon; Suburban Mansion: Beat-Hulk

DriveSwing homeStead.
FingerStab doorRaise.
TingleStress scalpWrinkle.
ScrapeBeemer.
GoneVette.
SwingPark nineReady.
StillHall.
DoorSwing kitchenWalk. FoodSmear fridgeArt:

G O R T !
K L A A T U
B A R A D A
F U C K Y O U !

MedicGauze kitchenLitter.
HoleLeather chairHung jacketShuck.
TVRumble boomBelow.
SqueezePistol.
CautionDown stairSteal.
BlueFlicker recRoom.
WarScape soundBlare digiTV gameTableau.
BoySplay couchSet. EyeWide.
HeadHole redDot. SmallBore backSkull.
JoyStick thumbPoise gameEternal.
UpStair.
TrashBag. BackPack.

UpStair bedRoom vacantScene. FemmeClothes bareCloset.
SpeedPack.
BagShoe. BagClothe. BoxPaper.
DownStair. DeathCouch. OffGame.
PolyFilm bodyWrap.
FridgeWipe.
LoadLincoln.
ColdDrive.
EyeFront headBlank autoSteer.
ColdDrive.
TransBurb driveTrack fleeFlight.
ColdDrive.
WheelGrip knuckleBlanch tightMouth.
ColdDrive.
SquawkBlare. ColdDrive. SquawkBlare.
You in the Lincoln suv. *CackleBuzz.* Pull over!
MindSnap. RearView redBlue cruiserFlash.
SquawkBlare.
EyeScan roadRoute.
BrakeLight glareAlarm. PoliceVan frontBlock.
CurbStop.
DuoUniform sidleSide. WindowRap.
ButtonPush downWindow. Constable Paquette.
Gorton. Good do see you again.
What's the deal?
You're all of a sudden impordant as all ged out. Doen ass
me why.
Oh?
Suparerintendand wands do dalk do you.
Who?
Ged oud of da car Gorton.
I can't.
You can.
I can't leave it here.
We will watch it for you.

Like hell.
No rilly you mus belive.
I'll drive it wherever you lead me.
Ged da fuck out of da car Gorton.
SwivelNeck.
TrioOfficer standCombat GlockTrain launchReady.
I'm gonna lock it up.
Mais oui.
Nobody better fuck with it.
We will watch it.
WindowWind. Fucken better.
DoorSwing.
StepCurb.
DoorSlam aimKey chirpLock.
Right dis way.
In a fucken copcar?
Pardonez moi. Our limo zervace god cut Gorton.
Fucken comedian.
I will ave do ass you do lean over it firse.
Frisk? Whatyya arrestin me?
No. Bud everyone oo gets do ride in a bolice unit ass do
submit do a weabons check firse.
No fucken way.
NodFurrow.
TrioUniform gripTeam quickSeize.
Doen urt im doo much.
You fucken assholes.
RoughHand bodyFrisk.
What is dis Gort?
What's it fucken look like pig?
Id looks like a Taurus nine millimetre semi audomatic
angun. Purdy new doo. *SniffMetal.* Dough it as been used re-
cently. No doud aboud dat.
Congratulations. You know your fucken guns.
We are bartial do Glocks ourselves.

Look Paquette. What the fuck's goin on?

Jus ged into da car Gorton.

SubGround cruiserPark.

ClaspEscort prisonerTrek.

ThroughDoor hallWay.

ThroughDoor.

DoorOpen manTrap. DoorClose.

ManTrap.

DoorOpen.

NoAir questionRoom.

ChairTable solidCell mirrorWall.

Siddown Gort.

Thanks.

Inspector will be in ere in a segond.

Can't wait.

OpenDoor. MiddleAge sportJacket.

HeadNod. You can leave us Constable.

Yezzir.

DoorOpen doorClose.

GreyHair chairSwing legStraddle.

PullSpectacle paperWield. Let me read a list out to you. *Eye-Rub.*

Hi. How are you?

Just listen punk.

Wastea breath.

Bonnie Peters. Ann Jackson. Chantal DeAlbrecht. Familiar?

Readin the phone book?

Sally Reynolds. Karen Findley. Lucy George. Margaret Gut-teridge. Any twigs?

Nope.

Crystal Pantages?

ShrugSneer.

She's one you guys killed the other night. The others have been gone weeks. Months. A couple for a year or so.

Fucked if I know what yer talkin about cop.

Oh come now. Throw your mind back a few days. Or weeks.

I'll throw nothin. Where's my lawyer?

Barbara Bolley. Jacqui Harrison. Daisy Sam.

QuietRoom.

Jeany Harack. Susan Pite. Chantal Delicia. We're pretty sure that last one is a stage name.

GlareStare.

Molly Greenhough. Megan Findlay. Janis Rutherford.

We can do this all day.

Damn close.

EyeRoll.

I got a list here twice as long as what I just read. And those are just the ones reported missing. If my guys got going on it I'll bet we come up with plenty more.

Good for your guys. Job security.

Oh we never worry about that. There'll always be people like you around Gort. You're our ultimate job security.

GlareStare.

So Gort. What did your man see?

What man?

When he was staking out your place.

What place?

He was there a whole night and two days. Must have seen something.

Yer makin this up.

Got a car missing?

Car?

You know what a car is don't you Gort? You get in it and turn the key and it goes.

Fuck off.

Gonna report it?

Report what?

Your baby Vette. I'd think you'd be pissed.

We're all adults.

Any bodies at home?

Bodies?

Well I guess you didn't get along with that snarky girlfriend very well anyway. Good riddance. But your boy. I mean sure he was a depraved sex deviant who was this close to being arrested in connection with the disappearance of a young girl from her highschool. Know anything about that Gort?

ShrugStare.

Gonna get rid of his corpse just like the others?

EyeBlank.

If you do it yourself be careful. Make sure he's all gone.

Whattya tellin me this for?

Don't want you to take a hit you don't need to take. Hell knows there's a dozen times a dozen you should take.

What in the fuck is all this about? I wanna see a lawyer.

Gort you have to do something about all these whores disappearing. Everybody knows about your little social club in PoCo. Everybody suspects what goes on there. I got Vancouver City on my ass. Sure it's their own problem. But I got a hell of a feeling it's going to be mine too pretty soon. They've got some community activist missing hooker task force crowd raising hell. Stopping traffic downtown. Got the natives all restless. Women's groups. Human rights. Et cetera cetera you name it. Not the kind of heat any department can stand for long.

Tell somebody who gives a flyin shit.

That's just it. We don't. But VPD's just a crotchhair away from calling a press conference and telling the world they think the hookers all disappeared into PoCo and never came back. Nobody knows what evidence they have in any substantial way. For damn sure they don't have an actionable case. But they plan to light a fire under us if we don't stand up and confess that maybe we got some rangatangs partying in our jurisdiction who might know where all these dumbass women went.

Hmm.

Damn right hmm.

Whattya want me ta do about it?

Put yourself in my place.

Get outta here.

Try it.

Hard to fucken do.

What are you talking about? You live my life every day.

How you figger?

You ride herd on a bunch of wild west cowboys charging around. Everybody's drinking and fucking like it's ancient Rome. An unruly crowd of independent mind and savage spirit. No order beyond the most basic. All in it for themselves. One or some of them start acting like they're going to live forever. They flout every law written down or otherwise. They become like gods. Beating their chests and pissing into the fire with animal abandon. But they're not gods Gort and you know it. They're just assholes like everybody else. They need a good dressing down. A slap in the face. Bullet in the gut. However whatever. You getting me?

Yer cops are like that?

You think if I didn't run this shop with a metal hand they'd enforce the laws like they should? Not take advantage of their authority? Follow procedure? Protect rights? Keep their hands and their dicks out of the cookie jar?

We all got problems.

Now you're getting it. And I'm telling you right now Gort. You have to help me help you.

How would I do that?

Stop the bacchanal. Rein in your apeshits. Live slightly above caveman level for a change. And come up with a plan to deal with this missing hooker situation.

What's that got to do with me?

I'm going to pretend I didn't hear that.

Pretend all you want. I donno what the fuck yer talkin about.

You don't have to worry about a recording of this conversation. It would hurt me more than it would ever hurt you.

I'm not worried about nothin.

Nevertheless. Listen carefully. I want the disappearance of individuals into your shitpit complex out on that farm to cease as of this moment. I want some explanation as to where the thirty or so that have gone away have ended up. An explanation. Understand? It doesn't have to be the truth. Just some kind of story. Most importantly I want a person or persons identified who might be primarily responsible for whatever happened or whatever you say happened. And I want access to them in a legal sense. That is I want them for the purpose of prosecution. This is where your story comes in. I want a case. Something we can go to court and get a conviction on. That means along with whatever fiction you come up with I want *corpus delicti*. Crime scenes. Weapons. Confessions. Eye witnesses. The whole deal. You listening?

Uh huh.

And I want all this in my back pocket quick as yesterday. Understand?

No.

If the excrement does hit the circulation device. And it sure as hell looks like it's going to. I want a neat clean complete and utterly plausible case ready to go that'll make the whole thing go away for everybody involved.

Everybody?

That's right Gort. Except of course whoever it is that actually did the goddamn killings. If you know who it is and want to hand him over. Or if you don't whoever the poor sap it is you select as your patsy. That'll be your biggest objective. Be careful about it. Shield yourself by all means. Protect your friends. But get me a guy. Any guy. A good guy. Good enough to nail.

EyeRoll. You gotta be crazy.

BroadGrimace. Neither here nor there Gort.

Whatever.

Are you refusing to go along here?

Whatta you think?

Fine. *HeadNod.*

DoorFling. DuoCop stickSquad.

SwingStick tagTeam.

EarWhack.

FloorStomp.

ArmCrunch.

FootKick.

That's fine.

BeaterBreath.

Get up Gort.

MoanCreak.

I said get up. *HeadNod.*

HardLift painHulk.

There you go. Sitting up feels fine eh?

Uhhh.

Well you should say. Now listen. *LipSnarl.* I didn't save your miserable hide from those psycho gunsels just for my personal amusement. You've got work to do. Roberto left you in charge. Now get to it.

Uhhh.

Don't screw it up.

Uhhh.

Yeah yeah. Roberto is cold meat. Everybody knows. Whoopee shit. The same rules apply. Comprende?

StoneStare stabGlare.

Good. Now get back to that beatup Lincoln of yours and go get that stiff you got in the back buried or burned or otherwise wiped off the planet so we can settle down and get down to business.

LATE AFTERNOON; HULK HQ: EARTH-BURN

Goodness me. You look a lot different than you did yesterday.

Slight run in with a business associate.

A pit bull?

No. Nevermind. Tell me what we got here.

Right down to business?

Right down to that chair there. Gimme a hand.

Of course. Shouldn't you be using a cane?

There's no broken bones.

You certainly can't tell that by looking. Have you seen a doctor?

Nevermind. To business. Whatta we got?

I had to fill in quite a bit. Imaginationwise. So many transactions are done in cash.

Don't worry about those.

Don't worry. How can I get you a clear picture if I don't know where from and how much? It's the major cashflow. I mean. It's like there's money coming from outer space. Take this one. A drycleaning company just doesn't get the kind of capitalization that Speedy OneDay has. For just one example. What does a half million-a-year gross three-person operation need with five hundred thousand in the bank? And they started with three hundred thousand. And they only operate eight hours a day. It's wonky.

Sounds good.

Not even the most coerced tax accountant would ever agree.

Nevermind that. How does everything else look?

Well I'll have to spend more time. Days. But everything is running in top form if profit is your only yardstick.

It is.

Why am I not surprised? Well you better get somebody to look deeper if you don't want certain government departments down your neck. Employment standards for example. I think the restaurant workers in your Chinatown places are being abused.

So?

It used to be something you could get away with. But take my word for it not everybody does anymore. As soon as they're off the boat they get sat down by some immigrant labour activist or another and made aware of their rights. They're all scared stiff of course. But sooner or later you're going to get somebody with courage who calls the right people and starts to raise a fuss.

No problem.

Then there's the construction and roofing companies. It's rather community minded of you to hire straight out of prison but that kind of across the board policy is bound to get you in trouble eventually. If not from all the criminality standing around but for the dangerous working conditions. I mean. You've had several WorkSafe investigations as it is. And the cash payment schedules I saw seem to indicate that for some reason Roberto paid off some people. There are many of those with no names attached. And then mysteriously there are all these dropped claims. Undetermined payouts. Et cetera. I couldn't trace through these bank records all the way. So much is obscured.

Don't worry about it.

You keep saying that.

There's little or nothin ever written down. Never will.

If you say so.

Get used to it.

Well then I guess you have the substantial story. You have stacks of books here indicating lots of business activity. Enormous profits. Mysterious capitalizations. The problem seems to be where to stash all the cash without attracting either legal or income tax attention. Nothing much more to say.

I need you to especially confirm there's nothin there that couldn't in some kinda way be made to look like apple pie red-blooded straightjohn business.

That would be a stretch.

How much of one? Would a good lawyer help?

A good lawyer always helps. Along with some kind of accounting wiz. There's all kinds of ways to explain wonky accounts kept by amateurs.

We're not amateurs.

You are at business. That's your main defence if anybody like Revenue Canada starts asking. So don't wear it out.

I'm listenin.

And any auditor forensic or otherwise would wonder why you don't employ your own accountant.

Huh. Roberto took carea that.

Is he an accountant?

SnorkLaugh.

Was he an accountant?

Not effen likely.

Well. If you want to appear legitimate you're going to have to address the issue.

Okay I'm gettin it.

Glad to be of service.

Oh you haven't even started to service yet.

Oh?

Read up on all this stuff and start runnin things for me.

Running things?

It'll pay better than fucking.

I'll be the judge of that. You mean actually work for you in this. For lack of a better word. Company?

Yeah.

Do I get a contract?

Whattya mean?

Something written down.

By now you gotta know the answer to that one.

Hmmm. And where would I be working?

Move in right here.

Are you kidding? I've just spent the only time I'm ever going to spend in this poo shed. It's a wonder I got anything done. Thumpy heavy metal. Cracking snooker balls. Creepy guys hanging around.

Okay go downtown or wherever and set up shop.

Wherever?

Yeah. And come to think of it. First ordera bizness is I gotta list my house up for sale. See to it okay?

You have a house?

Not anymore. And I gotta find a spot.

A spot.

Yeah.

To live?

Yeah.

Hmmm. Let's ponder that.

Whattya mean?

I have to think about it.

What's ta think? Yer lookin for an office and a place for me to lay my head. Get goin.

Any objections to combining the two?

How so?

A livework studio suite.

Downtown?

Maybe. False Creek or Yaletown.

Jeeze. Kinda upscale no?

Why not? A man with your weight certainly suits it.

I think I hearda this Yaletown. New place. Crawlin with straightjohns. Walkin along with their poodles shittin on the sidewalk.

You'll live so far above that action you won't even smell it.

Hmmm.

Think on it.

I guess. *WarbleTone*. But we gotta get set up soon. *Warble-Tone*. I gotta get this. *PhoneStab*. Yeah.

Gort. Geek.

Yeah.

I'm here. And I'm not too fucken thrilled about it. It's morning. I'm never here in the morning. Fucken daylight is killin me. Whattya want me ta do?

Clear the fucken place out.

What? You mean the boozecan cash and receipts and shit?

I mean the whole fucken place. Call all the guys and tellem we don't go there no more. Take out all the stuff from the can. Box up all the booze and shovel it into your clubs. Get Friendly and his sister and brother to clean up the place. Take some crowbars and tear out all the walls in the hooker house. Then pull it off the property and put it on consignment at some RV place. Same with anything else that'll roll off. Rake over the firepit. Burn everythin that's lyin around. Bury everythin else.

What's with the scorched earth shit?

Nevermind right now. Just get the fucken place lookin like we never laid a foot on it.

Well fuck. That'll take some time.

Get at it and do it as fast as you can. Get Scroaty to call out his guys. They're the closest. And start scrapin the place.

Oh yeah. Scroaty. He showed up today.

Good.

Not so good. Had his ol lady wrapped up in the back of the Cherokee.

What?

He fucked er up when she started raggin on him about hangin with us. Right outta the hospital with a hole in his shoulder and the bitch picks her time to start seriously freakin on him. Still fucked up on painkillers.

So he beat er?

Parently. To death you wanna know the truth.

Aw fer fucksakes.

Effen wacko man.

And he just drove up and plopped her bod out from the back of the Jeep?

Yup. Pretty mentally fucked up too. Guess despite everythin else he actually had a thing for the broad. Fucken sad.

Has Friendly cut er up yet?

Nobody can find that guy right now.

Has anybody checked to see if she's even rilly fucken dead?

Well she might have been livin when he wrapped her up. But nobody could spend a night closed up in poly and still be breathin.

Fuck. Oh well I guess just lug er overta Friendly's work-shop.

Yeah we did. Two other bodies there already.

Get Friendly on the job ASAP.

That'll be a chore. Nobody's seen im. He's parently still runnin around all over town tryin to score shit for that junkie bitch of his.

Oh fuck is that the one who wanted the crack?

Think it's the same.

Didn't I give orders for her to be gone by now?

I think I remember but we got kinda busy. Besides. She actually is gone. He's servicing her offsite. Pretty thoroughly cuntstruck if you want my opinion. Since this broad took him on.

This whole thing is getting wildly fucked. We can't have guys drivin up and casually dumpin out their stiff girlfriends for free removal services. We can't have farmhands puttin out the word they want to buy drugs by the truckload to support their crazy whacked out bitch's dope habit. And we especially can't have wildrunnin crackwhores ravin away about that place to everybody they meet. Think for a fucken second.

I guess.

Wait'll the shit starts flyin and you'll do more than fucken guess. Now somebody find fucken Friendly and get him onto body removal right fucken now.

Gotcha.

And let's get on with it generally okay?

Yeah I guess.

What do I hafta tell ya? Take my word for it compadre. There's heat comin.

I kinda guessed.

Then you know why we gotta burn it to the ground. Now get goin.

StabPhone.

It sounds like I'm not the only one being moved around.

How much do you wanna know?

That sounds ominous.

I gotta have you in the picture if yer gonna do the books and run the bizness. But it's up to you how far into the other stuff you think you can handle.

There's no way to tell right now.

Okay then. Word of advice. Doen listen in on conversations that could getcha killed.

Afternoon; farm: GodHulk

BoozeFarm carPark.
Geeze Gort. *UtePeer.* They did a nice job.
Think so?
You can't see it. *HandRun paintSkin.* Bodymen these days.
Fucken wizards.
Fucken good thing if you have to park in a shitspot like this.
CanToss. Have onea these.
KneeSquat. Kaspoit! Not too bad at all. *FingerFeel.* But there's ·
this slight orangepeel here. And if you stand back in the right
light you can just pick up the difference in tint.
Aw fuck who cares? *SwillGulp.*
SwillGulp. Yeah fuck Geeksterman yer right.
On to more important shit.
Effen eh. How's the cleanup?
We got ridda the buildings this mornin.
No more hooker mobile?
Gonzo. And that old construction shack. Rolled off. We
crushed down and burned that decrepit outhouse and the tool-
shed and the gazebo out by the pit.
Good. Take me for a walk. Issat motors I hear?
Excavators.
Excavators?
They were in the big shed. I donno what the deal was.
I'm thinkin they were left over from when Roberto rented
em for Scroaty's grow op. Guess we never took em back.
No kiddin.
Oh well. Ours now I guess.
Whatthefuckever. They're comin in handy buryin all this
shit.
Fucken good innovation.

All except the neighbours are complainin.
What. Do we run these fuckers all night?
So far.
Well back off. We're in a hurry but not that bad a hurry.
Gotcha.
How bout the Quonsets out by the wrecking yard?
Too fucken hard to dismantle. We took everything out of
em and burned it in a pile.
I see the smoke.
Yeah it was pretty big. Burned like for three days. Still hot.
Okay and how bout the cars?
What? You mean Friendly's wrecks?
Yeah. Who the fuck knows where they came from?
Yeah but.
But we gotta make sure nobody left anything in em. Hell
there could be a body or two down there for all we know. And
weapons and drugs and stolen shit and every incriminating
other effen thing. Send some guys through em and pull out
the gloveboxes and trunks and burn any paper or clothes or
any other such shit that could be traced to anybody. Bad
enough they got their VIN numbers still on.
If there's any heat Friendly'll take it.
That's what I'm fucken afraid of. He'd spill in two seconds.
Well we'll do the best we can. But to like haul em all off?
There must be twothree fucken hundred of em. Take weeks.
Nevermind. Just do the cleanout like I said. The ruckmumps are set ta crash in here any fucken day.
How soon exackly?
Never can tell. Latest I heard they were set to blow the
whole case this week. Real heavy unorthodox shit. Any deals
we had with em are off for the time bein. They're gettin major
heat so we get major heat.
Well okay. I guess we can have everybody outta here by
midnight.
Sure?

Pretty close.

Good. I'll tryta influence the maintainers of the law until then..

Wow. *HulkSigh eyeSweep.* Some fucken downturn huh?

Could be worse.

Where we gonna congregate?

Good fucken question.

We had it prime here.

That's fer fucken sure.

Any prospects?

I'm workin on it. Maybe Maple Ridge. There's an acreage I seen on the internet.

That far out.

Fraid so.

The guys are gonna be pissed.

The guys can go piss up a shotgun.

Hyuk. Pressure's rilly getting to ya eh Gort?

You try keepin this op together. Even just in yer mind. So fucken complicated.

I guess.

Well I can testify. But. I donno. Things are hangin together irregardless.

Gettin a hold on it?

Good thing you put me onto Miss Powerpussy.

She workin out for ya?

I'll fucken say.

Well at least there's that.

Yeah we can't rilly complain. Considering.

Everything'd be supercool if it weren't for the Flamin Fucken Faggot Killers.

I'll tell the fucken world.

What a fucken pair.

Anybody seen em? Heard anythin?

Nope.

Still out there I guess.

Must be. But you'd figger they gotta get goin somewhere and get back to whoever can pay em and put em up. They musta gone back east.

Makes sense. Though fuck knows who's runnin things back there now and how they sit with whoever that is. Donno. Don't fucken know.

Who would?

What? Know where they are?

Yeah. Somebody must.

I been thinkin. Most likely the cops.

Rilly?

Well figger it through a little. They somehow find out where I live and camp out at my place for fucken days. Didn't care a shit about bein caught or nothin. Body lyin downstairs with their own bullet in it. Their own blood and bandages all over the place. Their own rental car in the fucken garage. Even left their own shotfullaholes jackets on the kitchen chairs. Tell me they don't have cop friends.

Chico and Flame got cop friends.

Fucken eh.

Just like us.

The only way it figgers.

Here comes Friendly.

Good. I wanna talk to that fucken loony.

Careful what you wish for. Fucken yack your ear off with all his holy shit. Off his fucken coconut the past week or so.

Anybody cleaned out his workshop?

Nobody can keep their lunch down. Can't even go in there with a fire hose. We're likely gonna have to torch the place.

Hey Friendly!

Gort.

C'mere.

I'll speak to you across this ditch Gort.

Actin kinda weird Friendly.

My choice. Across water our words might purify.

What?

Our acts might receive the sanctifying grace of natural cleansing Gort. I don't spect ya ta know anythin about that. But I do and it redeems my life.

Whatever. Clean out that workshop of yours. Okay?

You wish purification for your sins.

Huh?

Evil ways Gort. Like me. You wish to rid yerself of evil. But water and soap and scrubbin and scourin ain't gonna do it this time. Oh no. Not even industrial grade acid wash. No no no. We will require the sanctifying grace.

Quit yellin. Okay. Sanctify whatever the fuck you gotta sanctify but get that butcher shop of yours clean and sparkly before nightfall. Hear me?

Why did we kill em Gort?

Hush up.

Why?

You ravin loony!

All the death. As if we were God Gort. As if we had dominion over fate and the end of days.

What TV channel you been watchin?

It came to me during the final butchering Gort. I had a vision of you. Killin. Killin but usin my hands and my knives. Killin everyone all the time. Killin without purpose and feelin. Without nothin in yer mind but yerself. All the killin. And the naked women. Naked and dead. All over the place.

Speakina women. You got that skanka yers off the property yet?

I lost Maisie. She's gone.

That doesn't answer my question.

She's gone back into the druggy sewer from where she came Gort. *SobStop*. She's gone. I can't get er back. And it was so great to have er with me. So soft. She was naked with me Gort. Naked. And alive. Naked and alive not naked and dead like all the others you gave me. Why did you do that Gort? I'm askin ya now cuz I donno if I can ever face you again. I'm thinkin yer the Devil Gort. Are you the Devil?

You have fucken lost it buddy.

They were just people like you and me Gort. But now they're dead. And I miss every one of em. Even though I never knew most of em. I miss em. I dream about em. I feel like I knew em and loved em and woulda taken carea them if only I'da known em before they ran into you. Before they ran inta the devilish evil. It eats at my insides Gort. The world is less of a place without em. The loss and the emptiness of it all. Like my Maisie. Even like Sidewinder. Gone. All gone. All empty. Do you ever have that kind of a feelin Gort?

Just get your shop cleaned up.

Nothin will make it clean.

Try kerosene. Burn it down.

Not even the ternal firesa hell would ubsolve what we done here Gort.

BackTurn. How long has he been like this?

Well truth be told. He was always pretty wonky. We probly never shoulda leaned on him like we did.

We gotta get him off this property before the cops get hold of im. Fucken bug'll spill the whole shiteree.

That'll be tough. Poor fucken idiot grew up on this dirt.

Let's get outta here. Can't standim starin at us.

Gets to ya all right.

StrollMonster.

Gimme another onea those.

Here.

Kaspoit! Where the fuck is Scroaty?

Took off yesterday. After we drank near all the booze that was left in the can. Pretty darn good party.

Glad you guys are makin the best of things.

Aw well you know how it is man.

Yeah yeah. Was he goin back to his condo?

Naw. Figgers his ex's family'll be callin soon. Lookin for little daughter.

What'd he do? Beat the shit out of er onehanded?

Musta been somthin like that. I never seen the body.

Sonofabitch. He sure can pick his time.

Yeah. I guess we gotta lay low for a while.

Effen eh we gotta lay low. And the other thing we gotta do is we gotta finger some guy to take all this heat.

Whattya mean?

The cops want a fallguy.

Just a single sucker?

Sure. That'll do. Accordin to them.

A patsy.

Yup. Along with a credible story to go with im. Somethin they can use to charge the guy and then clog up the courts for years and years until the heat from all this shit blows over.

Who the fuck are we gonna get?

That's why I wanna talk to Scroaty. That's why I'm bringin it up with you. We gotta put our heads together.

Let's see.

It's gotta be a guy who knows this place. Been here. Left his piss and shit on the ground so to speak. Fucked at least wunner twoa the dead bitches. Has the sicko cred to do the stuff we're gonna make it out he does. Maybe got a record for related shit. But not too important. Nobody who knows anythin. Nobody who's runnin a major op or anythin like that. We can't afford the guy spillin about the whole operation. Anythin come to mind?

Not offhand.

Who was that guy we had watchin my place?

Dirtybird.

Whose guy is he?

Well he's mine mostly. That is if I'm still sposed to look after the docks and marine union.

If you were before you are now.

Okay. But Scroaty used to use him for security at those rave deals he was promoting.

Raves?

Years ago. He's been outta the business since those parents groups got up in arms.

So he works for you mostly.

Yup.

I know you told me before. What kinda guy is he again?

The usual. Big. Gross. Major porn collector.

You said he could look like a stockbroker.

That was years ago. Before he got his face pushed in doing rave security.

And we sent this fucken freak to stake out my house?

You were in a hurry.

No wonder the ruckmumps knew every move we made. We stuck a fucken monster out in plain public view. Fuck me.

Sorry man.

Sorry doesn't fucken cut it man. Stop sayin sorry. If yer gonna say anythin at least make it constructive. Okay?

Okay.

So help me think this through. Dirtybird.

If you wanna set im up as a stalkerslayer type maybe we can use the cop action outside your house. I mean. They actually saw the guy lurkin around and actin suspicious.

I'm likin it.

Okay.

Where's he live?

Onea our shithouses in East Van. Basement. Takes care of the rents upstairs.

Okay yer straight ahead opinion. Dispensable?

Dirtybird? Totally.

Okay in your mind does he fit the idea of a sicko bitchkiller?

If you could see his walls man. I was there one night for a

stag. Whacked out graffiti. s&m blowup dolls lyin around. Skin-
books. Crossbows. Chains. Guy lives like Charley Manson.

Okay soundin good. Can we get somethin over there to rilly
fucken nail the guy? Like a shovelfulla dirt from Friendly's
compost sprinkled in his garbagecan or somethin like that?

Hmmm. Feasible.

Okay get workin on it tootsweet eh. Sooner the fucken
better. Where's the guy right now?

Likely down on the waterfront somewhere.

Okay. Okay. Let me think.

Man this is gettin complicated.

Yer not fucken kiddin.

Evening; Yaletown: CopRule

PentHouse realtyTour.
Geeze Na. This is rilly somthin. What a fucken view!
At your feet you will survey all to whom you deal drugs and purvey sexual puerility.
Hah hah. I gotta have a dictionary talkin ta you.
I'll tone it down.
No no. Keep it up. Could use a little class.
Thank you. I think this place would be a perfect first step in that direction.
Elevator ride'll take some gettin used to.
Just close your eyes and count to thirty-four.
Jeeze it feels like a guy could get a nosebleed up here.
Come feel the breeze.
Whoa there's an outside?
Of course.
What street's that down there?
Pacific Boulevard.
And that one crossing it has to be Homer.
I think so.
Man does it ever look different from up here.
You can see Vancouver Island.
Whew I'm gonna get dizzy. Show me the resta the place.
Here we have the dining room. Living room. Another deck. Smaller. For those. Intimate. Business meetings.
Yeah like I'd have anya my quote unquote associates come to a pad like this. They'd think I'd gone straightjohn.
I doubt that. You have to be a criminal to live here.
What was the tally again?
With maid service and furnishings and extra parking it's eight thousand.

Whew. Never thought I'd be payin that kinda rent. Why don't I just buy it?

It's not for sale. Besides. Give it a try to see for sure you like it. The elevator might indeed drive you crazy.

We'll see.

And frankly I don't think you've got that much money.

I don't? Even with the Surrey house gone?

You don't quite have three point two five million lying around.

That what a place like this would go for?

The one across the hall went for that last month.

Sonofabee.

Just live here a while. If you like it I'm sure we can raise some other money.

We'll get creative. Right?

Easily and with purpose.

Baby. You're a broad after my own black heart.

I will take that as a compliment even though your terminology insults me two times in only one statement.

Aw c'mon.

Be quiet silly boy.

Hey. There are two master bedrooms it looks like.

One for you and one for me.

Aw c'mon ba—.

Thank you for not finishing calling me baby.

Are we gonna keep up this game much longer?

What game are you referring to?

Aw for fucksakes.

Do you want to know about the security features?

What? You mean the security features on your pussy?

You know about those. I mean the house here.

Sure. What kinda security does the place have?

Twenty-four hour concierge. Resident only elevator access. Security camera intercom surveillance. Motion detector alarm system throughout. The garage is video monitored. As well as double gated and motion detector equipped. You'll have to fill out this information sheet and attach a photograph and thumbprint scan for the building security staff.

Holy crap. Like I was applyin for a job or somethin.

I'm sure it's all for the good.

What if somebody tries to shoot me from an airplane?

Hide under the bed.

Ha ha.

RumblePound.

Whatthefuck issat?

RumblePound.

Sounds like someone at the door.

EchoSound.

Aren't we sposed to be alerted to somethin like that?

Perhaps it's the management.

DuoStroll.

RumblePound.

DoorWide.

InspectorGrin. Hello you two.

How the fuck'd you get up here?

Aren't you going to introduce me to the little lady?

Do I have to? Is it the law?

Of course not. Just polite.

Whattya want?

To talk.

Okay let's talk. Close the fucken door.

You must be paying a carload of cash for this place.

Just a rental. Come out to the deck. Maybe there won't be any bugs listenin in.

I'll get you gentlemen some refreshments.

Yeah get us a couplea beers.

Bugs Gort? Surely you don't think the police would have that kind of interest in you.

Oh fuck no. *DuoStroll.* Here. We can sit in the shade. It's fucken hot.

Wind is pretty brisk up here.

You get dizzy with heights?

No. Just in the presence of beautiful women. Who is that?

She's my accountant and don't have any fantasies about fucken er.

If I fuck her it won't be a fantasy.

How'd you like to take the fast way down? Over that rail there.

Gort I've got nine millimetres pointed at you and you'll notice I don't take my hand out of my pocket. The day I give a scuzzrat like you opportunity on me is the day I early retire. Now then. Have a little manners.

What the fuck you doin here?

CanServe. Here we are. Would you like anything to eat gentlemen?

Naw Na. Just find somethin ta do okay?

All right.

My lady. I didn't catch your name.

Na.

Perfect.

Thank you.

SlinkMove femmeExit.

I must say Gort. Watching her walk away is nearly as good as watching her approach.

All part of a wholesome lifestyle copper.

She bears further investigation. I'll say that much.

Speakin of sayin stuff. *Kaspoit!* Whatthe fuck is up?

Well actually I mainly wanted to congratulate you Gort.

For what?

The excellent job you did on that thing we were concerned about. We found the fellow all alone amongst all that tasty DNA. Firearms. Hatchets. Machetes. It was an evidenciary festival. Nice work. You found just the right man. Poor sucker started babbling biblical gibberish the minute the cuffs went on. Perfect nutjob. Hardly seemed to know what the hell was going on.

You got who?

Frederick Constantine Struthers.

Who?

Your crowd calls him Friendly.

Oh fuck. You got him?

Of course.

The guy's a flatout flake. Couldn't serialkill a box fulla flies.

Photo of him looks pretty scary. You can almost smell him.

Yeah there's that. But he'd never convince as a murder fanatic.

Your opinion.

He can barely tie his shoes. How's anybody gonna believe he did em all?

If we need an accomplice I like that brother of his. Stuart or Stewartson or Stewball or something like that. Besides. Why wouldn't they believe Struthers did it? He confessed.

Confessed?

You're acting like you're surprised by all this Gort. Didn't you put it together?

Well.

Don't answer. No need. By the time the crown attorneys get through with him he'll be the Son of the Son of Sam. We got the perfect witness. Saw him cutting up the bodies. Kind of a near girlfriend. Former and sometimes current junk crack coke you name it whore. Apparently knew him when they were kids and rediscovered him when she realized he was single and had a third share in a ten million dollar piece of real estate. A damnably neat wrapped up package I have to say. Fine work Gort. If I ever want somebody framed I know where to come.

What if they don't believe him?

What if who doesn't believe him?

A jury. A judge. Anybody with half a brain.

Look at the overall package Gort. The dirt alone. Groveling around with all those pigs. Who wouldn't believe this guy is bent?

Not if you look at it close.

Nobody's going to look at it close.

Doesn't make sense.

That's exactly why it'll work. None of this makes any sense. That's our most useful device.

Huh?

Nothing a whackedout Biblethumping serial killer does makes any realworld sense.

Hmmm. And the public at large? The newspapers? They'll buy this bullshit?

Look around you man.

Okay.

At this fantastic view. Just look at them.

Okay I'm lookin.

See it?

See what?

The mass ignorance. They watch TV news and believe it. Mass collective hypnotic ignorance. They're the most gullible dimwits you could ever ask for.

Oh.

I mean you broadcast that this idiot. Whattisname?

Friendly.

You broadcast that this Frederick something something or other is charged with killing tons of women. I mean look at him. One picture of this rummy on the TV news and the whole world is convinced he's guilty. Scuzzy dirtbag ignorant subterranean shitrat. You barely even have to put him on trial. And he's nutty enough to take the whole beef. Nobody else necessary. No interruption of trade. We sally on taking the profits like always and nobody's the wiser.

If you say so.

PonderBreath. Don't doubt it.

Okay. But if it was me I'd be makin sure he figgered out what his true situation is.

How do you mean?

I mean he's gonna be in there a long time and take my word for it he talks til the fucken cows come hometa roost. Sooner or later somebody's gonna listen to im and put three and three together.

Uh huh. Possibly.

Fucken probably.

What do propose we do about it?

Get somebody to talk to im. Get im ta understand that we can still make his family uncomfortable up to and includin dead if he tries to tell the truth. Or whatever he thinks is the truth.

Well he's already babbling that he cut up those women.

Which is about the only part of the truth that is the truth.

That's all we need. On TV he's a literal horrorboy. That slasher flick image. Family photos with him gutting the livestock. Hatchet in hand. This clown is Halloween Part Fifty-seven. He couldn't be more media guilty if he were wearing a goalie mask.

Even so. There's gonna be somebody askin questions.

Not if our courts have anything to do with it. The Crown'll be going for a publication ban right off the hop. All anybody's going to know is what they read in the papers. And after the info spigot gets turned off everything in the media will be mainly fiction if it isn't already. Our cops'll only develop evidence to convict the filthy slob. They're stretched anyway. No overtime. And you and I know damn well the rank and file police crowd is generally as dumb as the greater public anyway. Putting a scuzzrat like this in jail for life on general principle is a cop's dream.

Seems tied up.

That's because it is.

I can't hardly believe the world is this fucken clueless.

As long as you undertand that and use it to your advantage you'll always prosper.

Good to know.

But there's another thing.

What other thing?

We have this missing women thing pretty well tied up with your big offering. And I thank you again for that.

Don't mention it.

But now we have Surrey detachment investigating a school disappearance.

Somebody stole a school?

Funny boy. Now I know your kid is no longer around.

Uh huh.

You know anything about a Shanelle Christina Bolger? Young girl in a couple of his classes? Went missing nearly a month ago now?

Fuck no.

Funny thing is her aunt dropped out of sight shortly thereafter. She was acting as guardian for the kid.

Nothin to do with me.

Of course not. But if there ever was.

There won't be.

Don't be so sure.

Whatthefuck ya talkin about?

You're a careful man Gort. It's the reason you're still around.

Yeah.

But your boy wasn't. Not exactly a chip off the old blockhead.

GlareScowl.

Don't forget Gort. We had access to your house for a comfortable long time.

GlareStare.

Yes. Silence is probably the best position. For you. For everybody. For good.

I donno what yer talkin about.

Exactly. And I know that our business relationship in that respect is solid my lad. Mutual backscratch. Mutual assured

destruction. We are mutually attached and mutually cooperative and that's as it should be and as it should stay.

So?

So as just that much of an added incentive my lad. Just so
you never go thinking perhaps you don't need the old Inspector to insure your clear way in the world. Surrey detachment
only knows about you as a lately relocated organized criminal
boil off their collective asses. Through my influence they will
be disinclined to investigate the Bolger matter in your direction.

But if.

Precisely my boy. If.

If?

You should ever stray.

Fuck off. You gonna touch that beer?

I'm a twofisted drinker. I only have one fist to play with.
And besides. My aim goes off under the influence.

I gotta take a piss. Jump over that fucken rail while I'm
gone. Okay?

Hah. Good boy.

Afternoon; hulk HQ: ThinkPain

ClubChair monsterSummit.
So it's lookin like the cops are pretty much runnin things.
Rilly?
Fucken rilly. *Kaspoit!* You shoulda seen the way they
scooped me off the fucken street. Like the goddamn CIA.
Way outsteppin their authority.
Like fucken Nazi Germany man.
What's the fucken world comin to?
Effen precisely man. This whole civilization thing collapses
if you can't trust the fucken cops.
Who is it exactly?
Some fucken Inspector. Roberto might have known his
name. He never gave it to me.
You saw him?
He fucken kidnapped my ass. Yacked at me til I was damn
near deaf. Then laid on a jailhouse lickin. Two fucken cops
swingin nightsticks. That wasn't fucken outrageous enough
he practically home invaded my new hideout.
Hey when we gonna get a invite for the housewarmin?
My fucken social calendar's kinda clogged up right now
Scroaty. I mean with tryin to get a handhold on all this bizness
Roberto left hangin and gettin myself settled after that PoCo
abortion and losin my family. Pullin up stakes at the farm.
And now this berserkicide cop.
We got any pull on this maniac?
I donno Geek. I'm havin trouble thinkin straight.
Nevermind the fucken ruckmumps. Where the fucker
those cornhole killers?
Yer guess is fucken good as mine.
Nevermind those assholes. They got no interest over here

anymore except revenge. Nobody's payin em. That's the main thing. My money's on they've already blown town. Hitchin back to frogland by now I'll lay odds. Forget em.

Look it doesn't help. All this bullshittin. Let's get down to brass nails here. How do we get a rein on this haywire Inspector?

Hardly anybody even knows what the fucken guy looks like. Keeps himself pretty well insulated. So it'll have to be somethin he wants. Forget about gettin somethin he dreads.

Good thinkin Geek. Whatta we got in that department?

Well there's the big shootout up at Rudy's place out in the canyon there a few months ago. They're callin it the Toolshed Killings. Cops still don't know for sure who whacked those four ruckmumps. Nobody thinks Rudy coulda done it all by himself.

So whatta we know about it? For sure I mean.

Does it fucken matter? We let this Inspector know we know who did the Toolshed Killings. We'll let him in on it if he calms down and starts acting like the secondary figure he is in this whole thing. If he bites we hand him Chico and Flame.

How do we hand him Chico and Flame? We haven't got the fucken slightest idea where the fuck they are.

We wait a while. Let things simmer down. Put the word out around here and back east that all is forgiven. We want to put things right. We dangle some green. Offer a peace payment. That'll smoke em out.

If only so they think they can whack us. As well as take our money.

We'll be ready.

I'm liken it.

Sounds like its got potential to me.

Okay so I'm seein the possibilities here but seriously. You guys rilly gotta see this fucken fiend for yourself. This Inspector guy. Fucken monster.

Big?

No no. Kinda small actually. No I mean mean. Powerglad. Knows how to swing the stick at the most painful spot if you know what I'm sayin. I'm thinkin if he doesn't bite on the Toolshed Killers bait we gotta have somethin in our other pocket that'll be sure to fuck im up. If not for real at least mentally.

I donno man. He's ridin pretty high on this missing women thing. Big fucken hero. Got Friendly all trussed up like a Christmas turkey.

Yeah yeah. But that whole deal is so fulla holes.

God it was such a fucken laugh when they swooped down. Whooda thunk they'd rank and guzzle ol Friendly for the beef? I mean. I had all the gear packed up and ready to frame fucken Dirtybird. That sure was a close one.

You what?

I had all the garbage you talked about. Dirt and all that. To shove in his trashcan. You know.

You still got that stuff?

Uh huh.

Well yer not as fucken smart as I was beginning to think Geekster. You shoulda got ridda that shit by now.

I know I know. Been kinda busy.

But I'm glad you still got it.

Yeah?

Why don't we keep it somewhere safe in case the Inspector's men need a mind fucking?

Wow man. That's freakin.

Creativity I think they call it.

Yeah ya know I'm thinkin all the time about what we gotta do to restore order and get goin back on a level road here. You guys gotta help.

Okay man.

Solid baby.

Okay. What's next on the agenda? How's bizness goin?

Fine.

Okay.

Right. Hmmm. There's something I was thinkin about but I forgot what it was.

Aw man don't think too hard. It'll shrink yer brain.

That's it! Small brain. Friendly. Somebody's gotta get into that jail and let him know he can't start tellin the truth or there's gonna be shit to spray. We'll get his miserable family and him too.

Good plan.

Yeah. A definite loose end.

Who we got ta handle it?

I donno. Guess we could get a guy ranked on some bum beef.

That'd mean a volunteer.

Morale is the shits. I doubt we could find a guy.

Some other angle.

Nobody visiting the guy?

Only Rosa.

Refresh my rusty memory. Whoodda fuck is Rosa?

Dontcha remember? We almost stuck a blade up er snatch.

Oh fuck. The sister.

Yeah.

Well somebody go and have a talk with er. And Stew too. Cops think they'll sweat him if they need a co-conspirator. Let him know we'll dick im up good if he tries to spill what happened.

Who you want for that job?

You better do it Geek. You got a way with personnel management.

Thanks for the fucken compliment.

But don't get seen doin it.

Why not?

I don't like the way the cops are goin outta their way lettin us know they think this thing is tied up in a pretty ribbon. Don't buy it all the way. I mean. Maybe they are that lazy. I don't

know. But don't take any chances gettin seen layin heat on witnesses. Or talkin into a wire. Or anyfuckenthing like that.

Gotcha.

Fuck. Where's another beer around this place?

In the fucken fridge Scroaty where ya fucken think? Get
one for me.

And me.

Okay you fucken guys.

Yer a helluva waiter Scroat.

Afternoon; public safety building: SexWeapon

StaleAir questionRoom.
Na. What an honour. Please sit.
ChairTable solidCell mirrorWall.
Thank you. I think.
Wondering why I grabbed you here?
I'm sure you have an excellent reason.
Always.
It never occurred to me that police vehicles could be dedicated to chauffeuring.
You'd be surprised.
I'm sure. Now perhaps you might indeed tell me why I'm here.
You're running things for Gort.
Are you certain?
I know what I know.
You and I have only met once and I don't believe we had a conversation. We were not even properly introduced.
I don't need conversation to find things out.
Then I assume you're the phantom authority he speaks of.
He's better off keeping his trap shut if he knows what's good in the world.
Oh don't worry. There's never a name. No specifics. Just this faceless omniscient presence in the background.
You're not so bad yourself from what I hear. As an omniscient presence I mean. Got full rein on all the legit money-washing enterprises. Amazing. These assholes don't even trust themselves. For a lady to take over. And an offcolour one at that. You must be something special.

My mother always thought so. But otherwise I'm just an underemployed business school grad who's fallen among thieves.

And killers rapists drugdealers slavetraders bootleggers strongarmers and embezzlers. Thieves is considerably down the list. All round low rent gangsters is what they truly are.

Perhaps I can raise their game a little.

I'm sure you can. Hope so too. It's in all our interests.

Of course.

You know my arrangement?

Are you the column in all the books listed as miscellaneous?

Is that what they call me? Yeah I suppose so. In the legit stuff. I get ten points of everything else.

Everything else.

The off the books stuff.

I see.

Can you negotiate?

What do you mean?

You know. Talk back and forth. Bargain. Deal.

That depends.

Whatever. Tell Gort the new game is twenty percent. And ten more on the miscellaneous.

You want a raise.

I want to be a bigger. Participant.

Participant?

Yes.

From what I've seen you've never been more than a piece of hired insurance. An employee if you will.

Look lady I bring you in here politely like a gentleman and talk to you in a civil manner. That could change.

You don't consider yourself an employee.

Not hardly.

In fact it is an insult. Asking for a raise would be common. Coarse. Much as an employee would be if you were one.

Exactly.

Please accept apologies.

Accepted.

You consider yourself an owner.

Partner. How's that?

Fine. Though I never found an incorporation charter any-where. No bylaws.

Everything's informal and you know it.

Actually Gort made me aware that you might be speaking in this way. Subsequent to the recent. Change.

He got rid of Roberto. Nice move.

Immaterial to me. I wasn't around during the previous regime.

Good for you.

But there were certain arrangements made.

What are you talking about?

In addition to Roberto's prudent assignment of Gort to run the operation in his absence. He equipped Gort or his agent to deal with you in the event of any untoward injury or request and or especially an unwarranted demand for increased con-sideration.

What in hell are you talking about?

Do you mind if I reach into my bag?

Go ahead.

PaperRustle. Please read this.

Hmmm. *SpectacleMount*. Hmmm. Interesting. *DownSpec-tacle*. Hmmm.

You'll agree that it is comprehensive.

Hmmm.

Almost eerily prescient as to this meeting and your current demands.

The original is somewhere I would never find it.

Of course.

And in the case of any kind of intervention.

Released to authorities beyond your sphere of influence. Of course.

Hmmm. *ReSpectacle*. Well I'll be. Says here Carlo Antonio DiCico.

AKA Chico.

Also AKA Triple O I'm told. And the Italian Rapscallion. But only in Ontario.

How colourful.

Yeah. *SquintRead*. And Francis Xavier Luminati.

Commonly known as Flame.

So that's their official monikers. These guys play on their nicknames as if Jesus H. Christ anointed them. Most times you can win the lottery easier than find out what it says on their birth certificates. Comes in handy for non-identification purposes. Perfect for outlaws. Keeps us cops guessing around in circles. But here Roberto acts with circumspection even as he speaks from the grave. Did a lot of homework it looks like.

Much to Gort's benefit.

It seems.

My impression is that this Roberto was essentially a family man.

An apt assessment.

Certainly took care of his own.

On that subject. Just so we're clear. *PaperShake*. This is somewhere absolutely safe?

Relax Mister Inspector. No one will know of your tawdry affair with a young probation officer and its fatal termination at the hands of hired killers.

Since you seem like such a pistol yourself. I'll take your word on that.

As you should.

As I must.

But I would remark. Such ruthlessness to deal with an otherwise mundane circumstance. Killing some little girl. And while on the job no less. And a distasteful job it must have been. I only just recently met this Skutowski character. Gross. And just because she threatened to foul your perfect little regime.

We're just like you people. No difference.

How so?

We don't let anybody get in our way.

I cannot speak from much experience. I admire your shaping the event to appear work related. Though with the connections you must have it might not have been too much effort. Still. From what I have seen of Gort and his friends and their methods. If you are speaking of savagery I must say you are all on a certain plateau by yourselves.

It doesn't matter. Gangster. Squarejohn. Politician.

Well then. Since we are all birds of a feather. Unless somehow relations between us deteriorate to an untenable state you have nothing to worry about.

You have a lot of power. *RaisePaper*. Here.

It's all relative. We still very much require the cooperation of the police.

Us guys? With a letter like this you could cut a wide detour around.

We still need the pretence.

Aha. I see. You know far more than you'd like me to know you know.

How so?

You know the game.

Please explain it to me.

You pretend to make friends with us and we pretend to fall in love with you. We trade info. We sabotage each other with false intel. We do the usual press briefings to say everything is under control. You keep it to a civilized level and cut us in so we let things go by. All is quiet. All is prosperous. All a joyous game.

However you wish to characterize it.

And you still need that huh?

Better to be on the safe side. Yes?

At the going rate?

We're not greedy.

With this letter you could squeeze.

Are you impressed that we are not?

Hah hah. You are some babe.

I take that as a compliment.

It looks like the power is in the right hands.

Perhaps. But Gort is the key. And things are not as good as they could be. I don't know if you know. His life expectancy is sketchy at best.

The killers? Yeah. They don't appreciate Gort's brand of inhospitality.

Gort has never fully apprised me of the events.

Well he and a couple of other yahoos tried to shoot these guys. All they did was make a lot of noise and get Gort's suv banged up.

A bizarre scenario.

That's not the half of it.

How do you mean?

You know they killed his family? His kid at least. His girl-friend is missing and presumed violated and likely dumped on a roadside somewhere.

I did not.

Nasty boys these.

When did this happen?

Wait a minute. *StareGaze*. What kind of question is that?

A simple one.

You didn't even know. Did you?

I did not know what?

That he had an old lady and a kid.

I sensed it.

You sensed it. So in actuality you're just feeling your way here.

How do you mean?

Maybe I'm overestimating you.

I don't know what we're talking about.

My point exactly. Do you need to be told what all your boyfriend is into?

I wouldn't use the term boyfriend.

Whatever. He keeps it all pretty much under his hat I take it.

He never wears a hat.

Hah. Amazing. He gets you to run things but doesn't tell you what kind of mess you're wallowing in.

You're being really quite mystifying.

Do you know all the stuff about the can?

Can?

The boozecan.

Is that the place they keep the records and the bar and pool table?

No no that's the club compound. No they had a spread out there in the sticks. Not that you'll ever see it. Pretty much defunct from here on. But while it was going it was kind of a general shitrat nightclub crashpad whorehouse wreckingyard. The boys stood around a campfire. Drank. Sang songs like Kumbaya.

You're playing with me.

A little but not much. Do you know about the missing women?

StareSilence.

Aha. There's a lot of things he hasn't told you.

I choose not to say.

Kind of a lapse in communication between business partners wouldn't you agree?

Gort discloses what he must disclose.

I'll bet he'd disclose a helluva lot if he thought he could get you on board as more than just his accountant.

Whatever the case.

Whatever indeed. I'd look further into things if I were you. If only to know what to deny knowledge of.

That's just silly.

I'm a lot of things lady. Silly is never one of them.

Well. This has certainly turned unpleasant.

I apologize. Anything else you'd like to talk about?

We have heard nothing of Chico and Flame.

I wouldn't imagine you would.

But it is assumed they are around somewhere.

I wouldn't worry too much about that.

You can say this with assurance?

Let's say I can.

I suppose that's somewhat reassuring.

Consider yourself assured. Let's get off the subject shall we?

You are the interrogator.

I heard you're an unbelievable lay.

That sort of thing is relative.

That skirt barely covers your business.

If I'd known you were going to kidnap me today I would have dressed appropriately.

I get a scent near you.

You have quite the nose.

Could just be my imagination.

From what I understand you seldom rely on such indeterminate senses.

Hah. Good one. You're absolutely right. Still. Some presentation for a businesslady.

Sex is business. Don't you agree?

I heard you charge big.

Business.

Even for friends.

Do you do free police work?

But a grand per?

Yes.

Exorbitant. Even at the fact that you are so unbelievably fetching.

You are familiar with Gort and his friends. Would you have sex with any of those monsters for less?

I see what you mean.

And a fellow like Gort wants exclusivity. How outlandish is that? So he pays large. There's a price on everything.

How much for a blowjob?

Five hundred.

A non-latex lay?

Thousands and thousands. And only after a full battery of tests and the appropriate supervised waiting period.

Sounds like marriage.

I say again. Everything has its price.

I donno. Seems outrageous all round.

Don't forget. For Gort I include business consultation. Basic accounting. Personal secretarial work. Social convening. Et cetera.

The et cetera. Including all these gangland shenanigans him and his boys have been up to lately?

I'm not entirely up on their. Misbehaviours.

They've been acting like it's Chicago in the twenties.

I'll assume that's some kind of historical reference to ill activities.

Ill activities. You are amusing.

I don't intend to be.

So you think they'll listen to you?

They seem willing to do as I suggest. So far.

Why I wonder? You're a woman. In other words a thing. In their darkest heart of blackness they consider you as negotiable as a used car.

I try to inject a transcendental influence.

I bet you do. Weaponized sex for one thing.

There's an array of methods.

You're quite the logician. Ever think about coming over to the other side?

What other side?

I take your meaning in this particular instance. But if things ever even out I'll keep you in mind for legitimate work.

Somehow I doubt that will ever factor in.

You never know. Like you say. Your employer might not live long. These homo killers can be unpredictable.

Who are you referring to?

Chico and Flame.

I wasn't aware of their sexuality.

Gay as daisies.

While such efficient killers.

You know it. Fags are the best.

Homosexual? You're sure?

You never met them?

No.

Well. If you did. I'm sure you'd sense their sexual kinkship with the psycho murdermen of history. You see the signs. Get the clues.

Excuse me?

You read history?

Asian mostly. You'll have to help me otherwise.

You don't know western history?

Not outside of what was taught in high school.

Huh. I guess you do need some help. I'm happy to oblige if you've got time.

What is it you wish me to know?

This might help you in your current line of work. There's a lot that goes on you have to comprehend with your gaydar on full power.

Oh?

Take Hitler for example.

World War Two. What has that got to do with what we were talking about?

Anybody can see Hitler was a gayboy. I mean come on. The suits. The leather. Décor. Suicidal girlfriends. That was the trouble with their whole plan. That's why their philoso-phy didn't effectively carry beyond their military spheres of influence. Every kraut I ever met was a fag.

Really now.

Maybe you just haven't been around sweetheart. It was the same with the Japanese. Only in reverse.

How so?

Hirohito thought Americans were gayboys. It was something about nonviolent imperialism. You don't get a Jap's respect by taking over without cutting some heads off. And supposedly the way Yanks act like women. At least compared to your average Samurai. So they bombed Pearl Harbour. Surprised as hell when the good old u.s. of a came back at them with hellfire and nuclear damnation.

This is all quite. Startling.

More than you know my lady. The whole Second World War was a fight between homos and heteros. Inadvertent or otherwise. Just take a good look at it. The Axis didn't hesitate to commit major extermination on anybody standing in the way of full homosexual party rights. And then the Allies didn't stop with just slapping the homos down when they finally woke to the threat. You get the firebombing of Dresden and a dozen other cities. Militarily irrelevant mass killing. Nothing political or strategic about these crimes. Just pure heterosexual versus homosexual paranoid hatred. Pretty blatant. History's biggest gay bashing. It's pretty plain once you do your thinking.

You seem fixated on ethnic origin as a precursor to sexual orientation.

Just look at the facts.

And yet both our fellows. Chico and Flame. Seem to be of Italian descent.

The original fascists. *SneerGrin.*

Well.

I mean don't get me wrong. Homos of any nationality are reasonably fine people as far as they generally go. But just don't put them in charge of anything.

And by your own example you're out to prove via personal object lesson that heterosexuals are just as bad?

Hardy har.

I'm glad you take my humour.

And your insult. Good thing you're so damn attractive.

Thank you.

But no. Seriously. By definition homos lack certain humane characteristics. They're intrinsically antifamily. Have to be. For example. Most gay boys I've ever been acquainted with treat women like pets. Ornaments. Nonserious. They in fact will admit that they've opted out of the whole manwoman paradigm. Too much refracted energy. Too much time taken trying to understand. Empathize. Cooperate. So you have a legion of fellows who willfully shuck a large part of their intrinsic humanity. I mean just extrapolate. What kind of world was Hitler leading up to?

You'll have to hold my hand on this.

Womanless. It would have been a globe made up of cavorting gayboys swishing from bathhouse to bistro to salon. Punctuated with cruelty. Women locked up in detention. Fascists are big on detention. Genetic and social engineering to establish the gay option as dominant. And only enough females left alive to keep the male factory going.

Fascinating.

There'd be no outlaws. Like your boyfriend.

How so?

Camps. Anybody who thought they were better than Hitler would be in a camp. Or executed by way of piano wire hanging. Or summarily whacked by squads of sadistic Chico and Flame replicants alternating murder with mutual wank sessions and celebratory cruising in flashy cars.

An austere landscape.

Damn right it's austere. Downright dystopian. I mean look around. Take J. Edgar Hoover if you want a police scenario.

This is turning truly bizarre.

You don't mind do you?

Would it matter if I did?

Well I hope you don't mind a little intellectual discussion. I don't get much of it.

Then please. Carry on.

J. Edgar. Damn near turned America into a fascist state controlled by the FBI. Him and his right-hand man and half the Department of Justice. Dicksuckers. Crossdressers. Turd-tappers. All manner of patented homosexual stereotypes.

You seem to have it all reasoned out.

Right you are.

Would you be terribly offended if I opined that you were insane?

Offended but not surprised. These revelations are challenging and terrifying.

And outrageous. I'm sure historians would have issues with the assessment of historical events based exclusively on sexuality.

Why?

It ignores the fact that people of samesex preference are maybe ten percent of the population or less. What are the rest of us doing while they take over the world? Sitting around watching TV?

Exactly my point. The complacency of the majority. If we don't watch out the fringes will take over. Government. Business. Art. Science.

Crime?

Not if we can help it.

So. You issue a call to action.

Yes I do as a matter of fact.

And this is why we sit talking now about our mutual participation in underworld enterprises?

Absolutely. Our small contribution to a larger advocacy for the dominant sexuality.

Crime.

Orderly. Controlled. Under the radar. Conducted so as to create the least number of victims possible. And most of all.

Heterosexual.

There you have it.

What an amazing progression.

Glad you like it.

I must admit it has a kind of mad logic.

And most of all it is the reasoning for operators like you and me and nitwits like Gort and Scroaty and Geekster to carry on and thrive.

To save civilization through a heterosexually focused criminality?

Exactly.

Working toward total heterosexual hegemony.

You've got it.

My goodness.

So on that subject.

What subject?

The predominance and ultimate triumph of boy on girl screwing.

Oh.

So on that subject. Would you consider a freebee? Just for the lecture.

I would but. I couldn't afford to let word get out.

It would be our big secret.

Still.

Thousand bucks.

Unless you prefer rape.

My lady I've never taken it forcefully or paid for it in my life.

You really think not?

Of course I'm aware of the principle of ancillary costs. And the tacit female acceptance of the inevitable. But formally. From a hooker.

I'm not a hooker.

That's getting hard to see.

You're finding out now.

So what would it take?
There are ways.
Don't toy with me.
Chico and Flame are still out there.
Gone away. I can assure you.
No you can't.
I guess we'll have to leave it there.
I prefer not to.
Well. You've set yourself a far objective.
Far or not.
So. What else have we to talk about?
You want to have sex with me.
Hugely.
You can.
That's good to hear.
But we leave nothing off the table.
Nothing.
No.
What have we left off the table?
What have we been talking about? Just now.
Homos and hets?
Business.
Aha.
Always business. Now. Terms?
Hmmm. Let me think on it.
Thirty seconds.
You are hard.
Aren't you?
A pun. I like that.
Decide.
Okay. *ArmCross*. I said okay.
This is your answer?
I agree to negotiate. What do you want? Besides money.
Chico and Flame.
No you don't.

Please don't patronize. You can see I am serious.

There's just a phone number.

I want it.

You'll have to memorize.

I can do that.

Okay here goes.

Stop. Have me first. Then give me the number. Let me use a phone. Then if the call is answered you can have me again.

Deal.

The table? Bendover?

Perfect.

Would you like me to strip? Or would you prefer to remove my panties with your own judicious hands.

Confirmed.

Evening; seawall: ParkDie

HulkMonster trioMeet.
DuskBound parkSit.
Fuck this is the shits Gort. We gotta get a place to relax.

Whattya mean? This is Stanleyfuckenpark. People come from miles around to hang here.

You know what I mean. My ass is gettin damp on this fucken lawn. *Kaspoit!* Ow my hand. Fucken twisttop.

Scroat the pussy.

Why couldn't you get cans? *PainShake.* Someathese fuckers are on too tight.

Fucken liquor store didn't have any.

My problem is wherethefuck we put the empties.

Aw c'mon Geek. Do like I do. *GlassToss.* You gotta be skilled mind you.

To throw a bottle in the water?

Try not to hit pedestrians on the seawall. *Kaspoit!* But aim close enough to scare em at the same time. Hyuk.

Hah. That sounds like fun I gotta admit. But these fucken bowling shirts.

You can go without leather for a change.

I doen wanna.

Jeeze you fucken guys. Coupla whiny bitches.

Speakina whinin. How's the sichiation these days with that haywire cop?

The Inspector? Yeah we got him under control.

We?

Na dealt with him.

Whoa. I want soma that action.

Well you'd hafta kidnap her like he did. And force er over a table like he did. Then I'd hafta killya like I'm gonna the

Inspector as soon as I figger out howta do it without gettin caught.

Fuck me. Issat what happened?

He brought her in. Tried to muscle us through her for more cash. He fucked her sure but she laid a mental beating on im.

How?

Blackmail.

The best kind.

What we got on im?

Somethin left over from Roberto.

Oh yeah. I guess we doen wanna know.

You doen wanna know.

Okay then. So everythin's cool?

Cold.

Effen eh. No wonder things have been goin so smooth lately.

Yeah everythin but this clubhouse problem. Any progress?

It's gonna be a while. It'll be outta town for fucken sure. Even then locals in these places are getting paranoida guys like us.

What the fuck's their problem? Whattsa matter with our donations to school basketball teams or toys for homeless kids at Christmas et cetera. Useta work like hot shit.

Not that easy anymore Geek.

What the fuck.

It mostly seemsta be this missing whores ballsup. They put a gag on the press but some word got out that guys like us were involved. I don't keep up on it but Na's clued in on all this shit. Our cop support is in danger accordin ta her. Then there's what she calls the optics. People get spooked by barbed wire fences. Spy cameras. Killdogs. Then there's the whole no-drugs-in-schools thing somea them are on. They don't like guns. Shootin. Motors. Fightin.

Fucken straightjohn motherfuckers do their fightin online.

Hyuk. *ChuckleSnort*. Fightin online is like racin in the special olympics. Know why? Even if you win you're still retarded.

Aw man I gotta get you hulks outta town soon. Or cheer ya up somehow. Fucken humour is so lowdown it's buried.

Fuck you Gort.

Fuck you Scroaty.

Fuck both you guys.

Fuck you Geek.

Aw fuck where can a guy take a piss?

Nevermind. Just hold it. Enjoy the scenery.

SeaWall gazeHulks. Kaspoit!

StrollCouple.

BottleToss. Effen eh. *Kaspoit!*

StopStroll.

So yeah. This fucken meetin sichiashun.

We're gonna hafta just move inta someplace and throw our weight that's all.

FrownFurrow. Hey!

FemmeTend fussBaby.

HardHulk freezeGlare.

Whatta you want?

Did you guys throw that beer bottle?

What beer bottle?

That one. Floating in the water. The one that just missed our heads.

Oh that one.

I can see you did.

So?

So what's the big idea?

Go way.

What's your trip dickweed?

Fuck you.

FurrowFemme sleevePull. Andrew.

I just can't believe some guys. Sitting around a public park and throwing glass in the water where it might cut some kid's foot. What goes on in your minds?

Take it easy. Andrew. Just forget it . . . Andrew.

Yeah. Be like a faggot and do like yer bitch tellsya.

Are you guys mental or what?

An-drew. *FemmePull*. Let's just go.

Sweetheart I want to talk with these guys.

It doesn't matter.

You just can't be such assholes. *StepCurb*. I can't move on from here until I see for myself that you don't rilly mean to maim children and piss off fellow citizens by making the park a hazardous waste dump. I mean. You look like reasonable guys. What would your friends at the bowling alley think? What's the deal? I just can't believe it.

Mind your own fucken bidnez and shut the fuck up.

Well the safety of children in the park is my business. Don't you agree?

You donno what yer doin.

I know that I'm doing my duty to try to understand why broken glass keeps turning up on Vancouver's beaches.

WallWalk peopleKnot.

Hey man. You better just keep on walkin. Like the resta the nice people.

Not until you guys explain to me what's going on. I gotta make some kind of sense out of this. I mean. You're sitting here illegally drinking. Nobody rilly cares as long as you don't make a mess. But endangering the general citizenry. You seem reasonably grown up. It's not even a matter of right and wrong but just human decency. What's the story?

RearHulk flingForce bottleBullet.

DuckDodge. I can't believe you just did that!

PopThud.

HeadTurn. Oh no!

FemmeProne babyClutch.

FemmeSide downCrouch.

EyeRoll.

RedSpew.

BabyWake saucerEye.

Help! Help!

Wall Walk couple Gape. Glimpse Monster. Quicken Step.

Fuck me this is the trouble with a public place Gort. John Q fucken Public.

It was all I could think of for tonight okay?

Warble Tone.

Hulk Hand grapple Phone.

Call 911! *Panic Shout.*

Thumb Jab pad Key. Hey. What's up?

Hulk Toss drip Empty. Serves you fucken right man. *Sea-Splash.*

Right the fuck on.

Whatta fucken dickhead.

Yeah. Yeah. Thanks for callin. Yeah. *Phone Fold.* Well fuck me stupid.

What? Who was it?

Na. News about Friendly. They're chargin im with multi-murder.

Effen eh!

Whatta fucken laugh.

Let's get outta here. *Rise Hulk.* I can't talk with this fucken dickweed wailin over his dead bitch.

Stroll Monster. She does look dead doesn't she.

Well that bottle was kinda full.

Nice throw Scroaty.

I been practicin.

Hulk Laugh.

So whattya wanna do?

Get more drinks.

Yeah but we gotta get the cars outta here.

Yeah. City cops'll wander by sooner or later.

And there's too many straightjohns around.

Yeah. *Hulk Leer.* Otherwise.

Yeah. Otherwise.

Fuck yeah.

He'd be fun ta kill.
By rights the guy should be dead. Talkin like that.
Donno what the fuck he thought he was doin.
Mental illness eh?
Only explanation.
What would we do with the kid?
Sink or fucken swim.
Hah hah.
Twisted man.
Effen eh.
GroupMonster diabloLaugh.

Late afternoon; penthouse: FemmeCharge

DeckDrink.
ViewHarbour sunRay eveCalm.
Hey Na baby.
SmartStep. Gort.
Whassup?
ChairSide flopTabloid fingerPoint. You nasty boys.
Oh. *RiflePage.* The new Harleys are here.
Not that dummy. This.
What?
This. "Woman Slain in Seawall Outrage. Infant cries in dead mother's arms."
Yeah. So?
You aholes.
How do you know it was us?
Am I stupid?
No. You're not.
Well then.
Quiet baby. I'm takin in the scenery. Everythin's okay.
Gort. I need you to be serious.
Serious. Everythin's serious with you.
How many of these have you had?
What?
These. *CanLift.*
Oh a bunch. I donno.
Are you sober enough to have a discussion?
Sure sure baby.
Look. If you want me to oversee things. If you want me to be effective. You have to be clear-headed and serious with me.

Okay okay. Whattya wanna be serious about babe.

First of all I'm at the end of my patience with the babe stuff.

Oh yeah. I forget.

You forget a lot of things.

That's what I got you for.

The smartest move you've made yet. But you better treat me better or it might turn into the dumbest.

Look. Babe. Leave the heavy stuff to guys like me okay. Guys like me an Scroaty an Geek. You handle the sensitive stuff.

It says here you and your guys were acting like aholes in the park. Spreading broken glass. Assaulted a man and killed his wife with a half-full beer bottle to the head. Sounds heavy all right.

HulkSigh. It wasn't broken glass.

What?

We weren't breaking the bottles. Okay? Now let's get off it.

What did you think you were doing?

Who the fuck cares what we were doing? We were doing what we were doing. It's not important what we do. We stand around and talk and drink beer. That's what we do. Away from distractions. Okay?

I'm sorry. *ShakeHead*. I'm having real trouble here.

With what?

With your foolishness. Jeopardizing a borderline legal business empire for the cheap thrill of beating up innocent civilians. I mean. I know you're no Einstein.

Who's he?

Exactly. But even a decerebrated idiot could see that what you thought you could get away with out in the back woods you'll never get away with in the second largest city park in North America.

Second largest? *SmirkHulk*. Where's the biggest?

Nevermind. I've been reading all this tourism material the government puts out.

Huh. Why waste your time?

Because Einstein you've said so yourself you'd rather be out of the shadow economy and go reasonably straight. Your own words. You go for the big money and you're free. Our nickel and dime stuff right now is fine but even all rolled together it's not the big money. There's too many mouths to feed. The secret is in funneling that flow into legit investments. Do you have any idea how much there is to be made in real estate investment around here?

A lot I guess. Look at this penthouse.

Precisely. The big money is all around you. If you don't blow it we can convert all this dirty cash into clean holdings. But it won't help if you and your quote unquote business associates are being tried for some useless murder.

Hmmm.

Hmmm. Well you should say so. Hmmm. The most eloquent thing you've said since I've known you.

Aw c'mon ba—

Stop!

Now just a fucken minute here. *UpSit eyeGlare*. This conversation has gotten way the fuck outta line.

How do you mean?

Don't take that fucken tone with me Na. I know you know a lotta stuff I don't know an you think you can see things I don't and you might be right but don't forget who's fucken boss around here eh. Don't forget who pulls the fucken strings. I mean for fucksakes. A guy needs a kind ear once in a while you know.

A kind ear.

Yeah. Somebody to talk to who's not trying to piss right back. Who'll just listen and nod their head. Who's not always criticizing all the time.

Do you not know the difference between antagonism and constructive debate?

I donno what the fuck yer talkin about and I suggest you

just be quiet here while I say my bit okay. *RedFurrow.* I'm
fucken pissed off.

I'm listening.

Good. Cuz I'm about ta fucken blow my top here. I mean.
If it's not the business stuff it's the personal stuff. It doesn't
ever fucken stop an it's drivin me up the fucken wall. Now I'm
glad you got the bizness shit under control. You handled the
Inspector and I'm a little pissed off you fucked him but I can
understand the circumstances. I'm gonna get that fucker his
due sometime here but I gotta think it through. No matter.
Doen worry about it. Nothin sloppy like that park thing. So
doen worry. It's not gonna fuck up the bizness. If it means
anythin to ya I'm sorry it happened. It was a fluky oneoff
shitty little chunka circumstance that never shoulda took place
and I regret it. Not that we weren't provoked. The fucken guy
had it comin fer not mindin his own bizness. But I'm not
denyin we were in the wrong.

Anyway. To stay on the subject. I'm extremely fucken grateful for your help in all this and I rilly wantcha ta stay and be
my b . . . be my helper and my honey and my ol lady. Okay. I
said it. I guess I said it before about every fucken day but
there I said it again. I know we can be a fucken great team.
Like. With your brains and my pull we can get stuff done
around here. You wanna get into real estate? Fine. We'll get
into real estate if you think it's a good idea. Tell you the truth I
didn't have any ideas at all beyond keepin what's there there. I
mean. Roberto didn't have no vision that I knew of. He was
just livin day to day like we are now. So if you got a longterm
strategy worked out fine lemme know what it is.

But what's rilly buggin me is obviously the way it is between you an me. You in your room me in mine. It's gotta
fucken stop and I'll tell you why. I can't fucken go on like this.
I gotta have some lovin you know. I'm not a rock. I know I act
like stone a lotta the time but I gotta have a time and a place
and a lady who I just let it all out with okay? I mean it just

builds up inside. That's what the real reason behind that park fuckup was about. I was set to kill. I coulda murdered every straightjohn walkin along that seawall. I coulda slammed that kidda theirs down on the tarmac. I'm so loaded up I could jump over that railing right now. I mean. You didn't see my house. You didn't see Lindas stuff all gone and every sign of her wiped off all mysterious and everything. And my boy. A hole in the back of his fucken head. Brains leakin out. A fucken hole in his head.

HulkStop.

BreezeRuffle.

GullScreech.

LowRumble mullTraffic.

LowSlant yellowSun.

So. So. *HulkSigh.* So you know what I'm sayin here? I gotta get somethin. If we're gonna go forward. We gotta hit a note here. We gotta get a yes on stuff. I'm not a rock. I want sumpm. I gotta get it. I can't stand it. I just can't.

Well. *ArmWrap headHug.* Finally.

Huh?

Finally you come out and say what's in your heart and not on your mind. Or your crotch.

Didya think I didn't have it in me?

I wondered.

Well. You can stop wonderin.

That's a relief. At least.

Whattya mean least?

Oh. You know. One less thing to think about. Whether you're human or not.

Hah ha.

That's the idea. Laugh it out. Here. *BlousePull.* Dry your eyes.

Thanks.

Just for the record. It's okay to let down once in a while. It's kind of touching to see a man get emotional. But don't make a habit of it.

Doh. *NoseBlow.* I won't.

Hey. I don't need a snotty teeshirt.

Sorry.

Tears are one thing but.

Yeah I guess it's kinda gross.

EyeLock.

Hah hah hah.

DuoLaugh.

Oh god it feels so fucken good to get stuff out.

Confession is good for the soul.

Yeah. I think I heard that one time.

Whether or not you've actually got a soul is another question.

Now come on.

Kidding. Silly.

Aw man. *SwillGulp.* Everything's better. Even this beer.

Good for you.

But I need another one.

And I'm just the one to get it for you.

Would you?

Of course Gortikins.

Hah ha.

GazeHulk.

BreezeBlow soft Ruffle hulk Hair.

Yeah. *PanoramaTake.* All fine.

ChimeKnell doorCall.

Na! *HulkShout.* Who the fuck can get into this place without callin up first?

It's probably building maintenance. *ShoutTalk.* I'm getting them to look at the hall bathroom.

Oh.

Can you get it? I have to change my shirt.

Oh for fuck sakes.

You can do it Gorty. If you try.

MoanRise. RumbleWalk.

MarbleHall entryWide.
HandleTwist doorSwing.
What the.
FlashMuzzle.
TwentyfiveBullet gutCentre.
Oof.
Hello Gort. *PistolSpeak.*
HulkSeize. GutFire. FistClench doorHold.
Yeah hello Gortyboy.
Uhhh.
He's only got two in him and look at all the drama.
He needs more.
Shall I proceed my friend? Or would you prefer to do the honours?
Chico my man. You got some dark sense of decorum.
Oh heck.
UniFire levelAim hulkGut shootFest.
GutWhap.
GutWhap.
You can let goa that doorknob anytime you like Gort. We're gonna keep fillin yer gut with lead until you do. *ShotSnap.*
Uh. *HulkClench.* Uh. *HandFlex.* Uh. *DownHulk marbleSlate fetalBall.* Uhhhhhhhhhh.
Now you might be thinking. *LiftStep overHulk.* If you can still think. If your small brain ever allowed you to think in the first place. You might be thinking Gort that we used these smallbore lightstocks in order not to make too much noise. And you'd be correct. And now that you're down on this fine polished stone floor here you're thinking it's time Chico and I dinged you in your limited little noggin and put this matter to a rest.
Ordinarily he'd be effen right. *DoorClose.*
I couldn't have said it better. Ordinarily.
MurderMen madLaugh.
Uhhhhhhhhhh.

WeaponHolster.
Uhhhhhhhhhh.
Whattya sayin there Gort?
MurderMan overStep.
BugEye writheHulk.
Hey nice place you got here. An thanks for lendin us your Vette. Sweet fucken ride man. Where's the ol lady?
Uhhhhhhhhhh.
Mind if we have a lookround?
Uhhhhhh.
Not makin much sense is he Flame?
Never did. You want my opinion on it.
Hah.
AmbleTour.
DeckLounge.
BeerCan coldSweat.
Hello boys.
Na. Hey.
Got beers for you.
Mighty nice.
LoungeSit.
Don't mind if I effen do. *Kaspoit!*
Kaspoit! Nice view.
Up here you can see everything.
Hah. *HulkGulp.*
No kiddin.
How's Gort?
Got a helluva gutache.
That's all?
He'll need an EMT.
Perfect.
Soon though. Or he won't.
That's fine too.
SeaGull screechFight. AirTumble.
WaterPlane takeOff rattleRumble.

Na. *FurrowBrow.* This was your specification no?

He's alive. Right?

Uh huh. But not for too darn long.

Let me worry about that.

Okay.

You got it just right.

Huh. *BeerGulp.*

StarePause.

Sufferin fuckjammer girl!

I suppose you might say that. Whatever it was that you might just have said.

There's no equivocation. *BeerSwill.* You're a flatout female sex organ lady.

Yeah. *LeerGrin.* What Flame just said. Ditto for me.

Manners boys. *GlowerGrin.* Watch yourselves.